T0151075

THREE STORIES BY EVELYN SHEFNER

Common Body,
Royal Bones

Coffee House Press :: Minneapolis :: 1987

Acknowlegments: The author thanks the editors of the following publications in which some of these works first appeared: *Carolina Quarterly* and *Creel*. The author is also grateful to the National Endowment for the Arts and the MacDowell Colony for encouragement and support.

Typeset by Peregrine Publications, St. Paul.

The publishers wish to thank the National Endowment for the Arts for a Small Press Assistance Grant which aided in the publication of this book.

Coffee House Press books are available to bookstores through our primary distributor: Consortium Book Sales and Distribution, 213 East Fourth Street, Saint Paul, Minnesota 55101. Our books are also available through all major library distributors and jobbers, and through most small press distributors, including Bookpeople, Bookslinger, Inland, Pacific Pipeline, and Small Press Distribution. For personal orders, catalogs or other information, write to: Coffee House Press, Post Office Box 10870, Minneapolis, Minnesota 55458.

Library of Congress Cataloging in Publication Data

Shefner, Evelyn,
    Common body, royal bones.

    Contents: The common body – Royal bones – Troubles of a tattooed king.
    I. Title.
PS3569.H392535C66 1987   813'.54   87-27761
ISBN 0-918273-33-1 (pbk. : alk. paper)

CONTENTS

THE COMMON BODY

1

THERE WAS A GIRL whom the world thought the world of and treated as the world does, in such cases, without the necessary grace, or attempt at concealment. If our girl had not been resourceful, with inborn good judgment and a few other useful qualities – though nothing apparently striking or exceptional – she might never have got by, to the extent she did. As it was, although things did not turn out for the best, she was fortunate and managed to avoid a worse ending.

Appearing at the beginning among a crew of impetuous boys, the only girl in a good-sized family, with some of them earlier and some arriving after – all in a heap surviving the usual family conditions of closeness and discontent, nothing settled for good, but constant struggling and imposed decrees of order – theirs perhaps a little poorer than other families, though not enough to make their childhood an actual burden or a misery: these then were the things, for a time, she knew.

An ordinary girl, coming into her life among ordinary people. Not so much different from others, or such differences as existed to be naturally explained; one girl making her way among all those rough and lively fellows, any differences to be attributed to this cause, explained away, then forgotten. A quiet person, a girl, usually allowing the others the outcome of the struggle, cheerfully relinquishing the ball or the toy, allowing the younger ones to invade and trample down her constructions and retreats, the houses and bowers and hideaways she put together for herself out of upside-down furniture and torn bedding. At the same time making herself known, at times wrestling and scrapping with the larger ones, but a favorite too, seated on the tallest brother's knee, smiling a round-faced secret smile, the baby twins pushing below her, pleading, clamoring, shouting.

Perhaps then it was this invariability of their lives and the fact they knew so few other people that made them, for so long, not suspect. One girl, growing up among all those boys, will hardly consider herself exceptional, or such point of exception as exists will be attributed to the obvious differences: a boy, a girl. And it will go on this way a long time, a family, a large family, making the most of their own company, fighting, playing, brawling among themselves, farther off from the town than other families, so again more thrown in on themselves and enjoying that too, eventually coming to view the occasional visitors whom the older ones bring home as intruders, unlicensed disturbers of the family ways. And the girl, too, will respect and advance this opinion, she will stay home with them, with her parents, all those teeming, quarrelsome others, quite contentedly; then later, moving a little farther off, will walk part of the way from school arm in arm with another girl, but they will separate and wave goodbye on the road before going the whole way, before she will have to take the step of entering their houses, or bringing them in.

Sitting at her desk, picking at her braids, twitching in the seat, bent over the blank paper, filling it with loving scrawl, eyeing the teacher at the front of the room, chewing her pencil, raising, then lowering her hand, at times too eager, at times reluctant – then the day over, throwing down the books, the papers, picking up the other books and papers to be taken home – then down the road, sometimes hand-in-hand with another small child, often alone – but always quite happily coming back to the house, the sounds, the people in it. So year after year the girl, the school, the other girls, the house, the older brothers who no longer show themselves around so often, who are beginning to be frequently absent, and when present less affectionate, forgetful, more aloof. But she herself never enough out of it, hardly away from it, not well enough acquainted with other people to understand in any way the facts of the case, to begin to suspect her own rare, uncomfortable, unexplainable, distressing, perhaps wonderful, as yet undiscovered difference.

A life coming into itself moves by quick starts and long slow stages. Long mornings, short noons, consequential, busy afternoons crammed with activities so pressing and vital the doer has no time to look around, to stop or evaluate; then evening, which can be delicately langorous, or dreary. Quite suddenly it was all changed – the patchy play-trampled yard, the holes that the dogs had dug, the tire hanging from the flaking sycamore tree, the back steps made dangerous by the ingenious kicking and hacking of small boys. The two oldest brothers married; moved not far away, but came back now only with wives, and then with their own small children, who were adored novelties, and caressable pets, not, in the old sense, family. Then, not so suddenly, the father died. Besides the mother, the girl was left at home with one older brother and the young twins; solemn children, now they were no longer babies grown quieter and retiring into their mirror world, sharing their troubles but with no one else, crouching for hours facing the identical other over some impromptu game, whose rules only they understood, or flicking from one to the other small spheres of clear or murky glass.

Then the one older brother still at home gets married too, takes a job far off this time, in another part of the country, a distant city from which nobody in the family has ever received a letter. Shortly thereafter the mother, suddenly, dies. The girl and the growing twins are left in the house, which is of course far too large for them now. This is a lonely and stressful time for the girl, who must get up very early, attend to the schoolboys' breakfasts and see them out of the house before getting ready, herself, for the job she has found in a store in town, not hard work but confining; coming home at the end of the day to buy food, to cook for herself and boys, concerned about them alone after school, regretful now that the family has never managed to find its way in and out of other people's homes.

A young man appears as a customer in the notions and variety store where the girl is employed. He drops in to buy this and that, never much at a time, but he does come in frequently and, before leaving, stops to hold a little conversation with her and the owner. He is a boy of the town and, if the family had known more people in the ordinary way, is someone the girl would have known. In a sense, she is acquainted with him already, because they have been to the same schools, have seen one another without really speaking at picnics and ball games and assemblies. However, now they are both out of school by a few years, and both employed (the young fellow in a machine shop), they find talking easier and also a strain. Still, he persists.

Sometimes before leaving, he says odd things to her, in a straight-faced, teasing way. "I saw you last night right after supper, when I took my mother to the station to go visit her sister. You were standing at the far end of the waiting room, and you were wearing a pink dress."

6

"But I didn't go out at all last night," she protested, finding it hard to believe he could concoct such outrageous things. "I came home straight from work and spent the evening putting up preserves."

"No matter," he answered. "I could have been mistaken. It looked like you, though. And I sure admired it – that was a pretty dress."

Long past supper time, after finishing canning the preserves with the reluctant help of the twins, she had cleared the dining-room table and had started cutting out a pink dress from a bolt-end that her employer had tossed across the counter to her, with a take-it-and-forget-about-it movement of his shoulders. The young man had followed her walking home with the gift under her arm! Annoyed by the intrusion, she turned away.

But other things he said at times were not so easily dismissed.

"I'm sorry you had a bad toothache all day Sunday," he said solicitously, coming in at the beginning of the week.

Her hand flew to the side of her jaw. "Why? How did you know? Who told you?"

"I can't honestly say who told me. Someone must have. I got on the trolley this morning and said to myself, too bad she was laid up with a toothache all yesterday – I hope it's better!"

"I'm seeing Dr. Rodgers after work tonight," she answered, lowering her head. "It was better when I woke, thank you, but I thought I ought to see to it."

But mostly they would talk of things that happened in their worlds: his mother, who was thinking of leaving town and moving in with her widowed sister, now that she'd had a satisfactory offer for the house; the letters the girl received from her brother off in Philadelphia, telling of this and that in the city life, to which he had grown accustomed. She did not mention to her new friend that this same brother also

7

occasionally startled her by bringing up the sort of unexplainable coincidence as did he at times. "Tom wrote that you'd been seeing a young fellow lately," the brother had written her. "Take care of yourself. Don't go off on lonely drives out of town! (Speaking as a man, I know what I'm talking about.) And I hope you are taking good care of Ma's old jewels and things. Don't be careless with them now. You may want them later."

Had the brother *seen* her snatch her hand away, pull too quickly back from the young man breathing over her only the Saturday before, when they stopped on the dirt road leading to the pond? Had he seen Ma's cameo ring, which she had put on because it went so well with the pink dress but which was too large for her finger, slide off her hand – seen it bounce and hide itself in the underbrush along the road? Had he known then that Carl had spent a good hour at least there on his knees, lighting match after match and sifting through the moss and dead leaves until quite miraculously after the last match was gone he had felt it, managed to distinguish this hard stone from the other small stones and pebbles lying around, and given it back to her – breathy and sweaty, he, she embarrassed and unreasonably contrite? The episode, in which both perhaps were at fault, had helped to bring them closer; they drove home without speaking much, but at her door turned to one another and kissed an affectionate good-night. Her brother, all the way off there, may not have approved, but how could he have possibly known?

Questions like these, though troublesome, were so much the least part of the troubles ordinary living brings that she tried not to give them too much weight. She was a steady, level-headed girl, and if people chose to have visions about her or to see her at times or places where she was not – or at least when she was not with them – well, she was not responsible for their visions and delusions. She kept her peace, tried to laugh away these things as they came up, assuming

they happened oftener than other people, out of embarrass-
ment or fear of being labeled superstitious, were willing to
admit. And even after she and Carl were married, when he
had moved into the big house and taken over her life and
the twins, who far from resenting him, seemed hardly to
know that he had arrived, they allowed him to interfere so
little with their activities – even then, when Carl would come
home from work, kiss her, go in and see the baby, who'd
had a fretful afternoon and was now lying asleep and scarlet-
cheeked, her hand tucked in her small mouth: bending over
to brush the hot forehead with his lips, Carl would whisper,
"I see you had a bad afternoon with her. The colic, was it?
Carrying her around, screeching for hours. No wonder you
look worn out!"

"But Carl," the young wife would question him, "it is true,
it happened, but *see*? How do you mean, see? If you know
it, then how do you know?"

"I *don't* know."

Her husband would invariably be puzzled, he was never
prepared for this simple question. After she had asked, he
would be silent and work his mustache with his lower lip.
He would be irritated. Apparently he preferred not to answer.
"I can't tell how I know," he'd finally throw off. "I was sitting at my lathe and seemed to see you for a second, and
it seemed you were worried because the baby was scream-
ing with colic, and you wondered if it was bad enough for
the doctor . . . I did seem to see for a minute, but no matter.
I'm hungry. Did you have a chance to put anything together
for supper?"

At times, envying this apparent gift of her husband and
others close to her, the young woman would do her best to
apply the same lesson. She would sit down and try to peer
into conditions at the machine shop – Carl had by then set
up his own small place – wondering whether an order he had
been counting on had come through, whether the new assis-

9

tant was working out well or arriving drunk again and therefore have to be told off, gotten rid of. She would sit, shutting away her small children's voices, and concentrate on her husband's face: was he satisfied and showing it or disappointed yet doing his best not to show it, or was he working up a righteous anger, preparatory to firing a man? But though she tried her hardest, abandoning for the moment the chores and errands pressing at the back of her mind, nothing, or very little, came through. Her guesses – and they were no more than that – were as likely to turn out wrong as right. Even when she managed to guess correctly, it was still guesswork – that she knew – not this other. She apparently had not the gift, it could be applied to her without her consent perhaps, but she had no means of applying it. Not even did she have it in her power, more than any other worried mother, to know at all times what her small children were up to, but she must drop things and rush off to the kitchen, the yard . . . No, others might be gifted, but their gifts would have to be practiced on her. She was their material and not the other way around. She was to be allowed no visions, was considered not deserving, an ordinary ungifted woman, holding her life together the best she could, year by year watching events fall into their predictable arrangements, having little power over them, giving in, not fighting it, drawing what hindsight lessons from life she was able, hoping for much, then less, growing a little older. If there was any special thing about her, she'd think at times – putting down the phone, fairly startled, after a call from one of her sisters-in-law who reported that someone had identified our woman at a given date at a hospital entrance in a distant city that she'd never visited – if she was in any way exceptional, it was because she was common material from which other people's notions, their blunted and unrefined visions, were from time to time spun out.

2

IN OTHER WAYS, their lives, hers and Carl's, moved ahead, in some ways carried on for the better. Two babies, one soon after the other, and both girls. The better so, our woman thinks, remembering that turmoil of sprawling, battering arms and fists, the torn and muddied clothes, the patches, the lost mittens and caps, remembering their mother worn out, all day stooping, retrieving from under beds, stirring large pots, never large enough to fill those reddened cheeks, to pacify those battle-spurred appetites. Our woman, looking at one, miniature and perfect in the cradle, and the other, tottering capriciously in checked pink and pink bows, decides, for her, these two, no more. From now on, they will have to be careful. As for the husband, he will have to be satisfied with daughters. If he feels the need for sons, there are the twins, already planted in the family. Unbuttoning her blouse for the one, coaxing the spoon dripping with warm cereal toward the turned-away face of the other, she thinks, in my case it will not be as hard. They say with girls it is so much easier.

Of course, with girls it is not so much easier. Too soon, climbing out of the cradle, sliding out of the high chair, pushing off the cereal bowl, slipping down the road. She has the hope that she may have won back in them the little girls whose hands she had dropped on the way home from school — but as she clutches, their warm small grip slides away from hers, too soon, skipping down the road into their own lives. And then Carl does not always understand, he is not a man who is always ready to answer their teasing caprices and dancing self-absorbed pleasures: self-absorbed himself, tired out at night, sinking back in his chair, holding up the town paper in hands with creases permanently stained by machine oil.

And her twin brothers — so soon, so surprisingly they decamp! So quickly they are grown and come into themselves, tall, well-combed, carefully dressed, carefully spoken, exceptional students, both, given the highest recommendations. They go off apparently quite contentedly on scholarships to two widely distant colleges, like two halves of a person splitting apart. From the far eastern and western limits of the country, each occasionally replies to the letters of the older sister, who helped bring him up, telling a little of what he is studying, planning. Neither implies he is very much in touch with the other, and neither boy ever indicates, hints, lets fall any special prevision or foreknowledge of the sister, back there.

But the daughters! Fiendish sprites, darling witchikins — from the moment they are able to stray short distances away from the mother, to graze slightly beyond her range, they will come dancing up and announce, "I think old Mrs. Peterson was up here visiting this afternoon."

"But, pussy cat, how did you know she was here? I think you must have been hiding in the bushes outside, watching."

"I was not. I was at Carol's, playing. I just came back."

"Then how did you know Mama had a visitor — I'm not saying I had! Tell me."

Stepping back, the child would protest coolly, "I *don't* know. I'm not sure. Didn't she come to our house? Let go, Mommy, you're hurting my hand."

She could never get any satisfaction out of them. They were outside her power. Running into the house after school, a child would demand breathlessly, "Did Aunt Susan invite us all to supper on Saturday?" "Are we having chocolate cake tonight?" "Am I getting a little red wagon for my birthday?"

"Well, then, I suppose you met your cousin Millie on the way, and she told you about the supper party?"

"No, I didn't, Mommy, I came right home."

"Sweetheart, admit you went in and peeked at the cake cooling in the pantry!"

"But I did not. You see, I just came in the door."

"Oh, dear, someone from Mr. Rattner's store saw you and let slip that I was in there looking at a wagon."

A seven-year-old would stare at her, out of eyes of an extraordinary blandness and incomprehension, trying to take in how a grown-up store clerk could accost a small child and willfully spoil a mother's birthday surprise, could betray a confidence about a present hesitantly decided on and a deposit paid only that afternoon —

"But what makes you think you *are* getting that red wagon?" the mother would ask cannily. Or, annoyed that she was reduced to dealing them craft and camouflage: "How do you know that somebody isn't buying a wagon for somebody else?"

The child, her innocence undamaged, would simply continue to stare and, before looking away, might murmur, "I don't know, I *thought* I was getting that red wagon for my birthday. Don't you want me to have a wagon?"

To the mother's confusion and undefined fear would be added contriteness over her manipulation of this small creature, plus a need to sweep the child up in her arms and assure her through tears, "Yes, my darling, if that is what you like, surely I or your Daddy will go down to the store tomorrow and put down a deposit on the best wagon we can find!" A promise the child would accept with no show of emotion. Before extricating herself, she might give the assurance "That's all right, then. I knew it all the time."

But difficult as things were between her and them, it got worse before, in the course of events, this special connectedness began wearing thin. There were times when the mother felt so burdened and confined, so driven and pent in by these children's unrelenting awareness of her, that she felt a horrifying desire to be rid of them, at the same time she was tormented by the suspicion that they might have some access to this desire, as well. Before the rope began to fray – and as the children's lives became remoter to her she also apparently became remoter to them, until whole weeks would pass without a child's confronting her with some accomplished fact, some word or deed completed outside their presences – she found herself thinking of these children as imps and changelings, nasty, malicious, unlovable, not hers, not Carl's. Sprung from the ground like inedible mushrooms, sharp-toothed serpents who glide up at night to steal milk from the cow: inhuman, burdensome ingrates left in her charge.

However, when in the years following the worst did seem to be over, when these children's pursuit and invasion of their mother began to let up and finally more or less vanish, then, then, she could step back from it a little and assure herself that it was not so unnatural for those close to her, her man and her children, to feel her with them at times when she was not there. What else and for whom else had she been living all these years, if not for those closest? First the brothers, then the widowed mother, then taking on the younger ones all by herself, then the husband, her own children, and eventually grandchildren: she had not had as much dealing with neighbors and friends as she might have liked, but had that opportunity arisen, she would surely have spread herself out there too, because her nature demanded it. Then why quarrel with the workings-out of her nature? Any more than quarrel with this long brilliant autumn, the drift of wind and cloud, the branch shadows momentarily cast on the white frame house that was always in need of a painting, as she went into the yard and stooped under the hazelnut tree, picking up the last windfalls of the season, and saw at the end of the block five little girls – her own among them – doing a dance over a pile of smouldering leaves. As the worried mother watched, the children whooped and leaped over the dull pyre, which was stirred to occasional brightness by a shift of wind. They took turns disappearing into the column of smoke, chanting as if skipping rope.

Feeling the cooling earth through the soles of her shoes, her hands full of hazelnuts and a few last oak leaves, the mother stood absorbed by the motion of whirling skirts, the flirtation with the flames, the rhythmic chanting. The dance seemed as much part of the irregularly patterned day as the jagged cloud shapes, the poignant smell of leaf mold that pulled her this way, then that, the crunch of dried sticks and fallen acorns underfoot.

After watching for a while, she went back into the house. The regular chanting followed, growing more excited and shrill. Still concerned for the children's safety but unwilling to spoil their pleasure, the mother was relieved when the singing stopped and feet came pounding up the path. Guessing that now the bonfire was out it would be food that they were after, not her so much as glasses of milk and handfuls of cookies that they would swallow down too fast before hurrying off to rejoin their friends. She set out the glasses and went into the pantry for the covered crock, efficiently, tidily, as if it were a job – relieved perhaps but also a little regretful, now that the need to be so intimately bound up with those she loved was becoming a safe matter of the past.

3

FEW THINGS, of course, can be safely put away, finally answered for, cut off. In the play of action and counteraction, it is difficult to say what definitely is past, what is presently arriving. Or which endings follow on from which beginnings. Who could have predicted, for example, that a war breaking out, as they tend to overseas, should in the course of time lead to a shortage of a tiny part that Carl's machine shop had specialized in producing all these years? That the government should contract to buy up as many of these as he could supply, pressing him to expand operations, to hire more men and keep shifts running night and day, making him more than ever absent-minded and distracted at home but also, almost in spite of himself, fairly well-off?

After that, compounding unexpected good fortune, who could have imagined that this same government should decide to build an air base on the site of their old house, that cavernous relic and insatiable money eater hated by every member of the family but until then impossible to let go of; so that gleefully disposing of house and land at a profit, they should abandon the leaky roof, the sagging porches, the linoleum-lined halls, the old-fashioned fixtures, all the outrageous inconveniences, and move into a smart comfortable house in town? And who would have guessed at the bad luck that should eventually flow in the same channels?

At the beginning, it seems all freshness and release. So many things to look for, to plan for, to bring into the house, to admire, arranged against walls and hitched into corners. The girls excited and happy, not only for their new home but the assurance that they will be able to go away to college when the time comes, not on scholarship like their uncles, but on the strength of their parents' success. This is a busy and happy time even for the father, and especially is it a happy time for the two girls and their mother.

Encouraged by her husband, who is now a man of substance in this little town, the employer of a number of its citizens, the mother joins garden clubs and parents' clubs. She plays bridge. She volunteers for war work, driving around buttoned into a brown tailor-made uniform, in a limousine with a red cross painted on the side, helping to collect the dark red vials that she can never, not even as she sees the vein draining into a tube with the donor stretched on a cot, convince herself are filled with human blood.

Tentatively she reaches out and tries other things. Doing her fall shopping in a nearby city, she is mildly amused when the saleslady, helping her into a dress, asks: "How did your husband like the two dresses you took home Friday? He must have approved, if he sent you back for more!"

"Lordy," our woman laughs, as soon as her face and arms are free, "you must be confusing me with someone else. I've never been in your store in my life. We live sixty-five miles away, and don't get up here all that often."

"You don't say."

The salesperson reached over and smoothed down the collar. Her long face was suddenly whisked free of expression. She backed up a little and watched her customer in the three-way glass. "We do see so many people," she explained tactfully. "But" – looking steadily in the mirror – "the face, the hair, the coloring, the size, and then you went right over and picked out the dress my customer said she wanted to think about for a few days before deciding . . ."

"Then you're saving this for someone else?"

"No, dear, go ahead and take it, if it's what you want. I'll make it right with the other lady, if she ever turns up."

Feeling like the crudest forger or impostor, subject to arrest at any minute for impersonation, our woman left the store with a package paid for with her husband's good money, which she could not be certain she had any right in possessing.

On the other hand, it seemed less unnatural that people, meeting her for the first time at club meetings, at evening parties, at savings bond drives, should frequently mix her up with one woman or other they had known before. After all, people were getting together so much these days, everybody was rubbing up against virtual strangers, people were arriving in town attracted by its new industries, and all was in a pleasant condition of turmoil, with Red Cross activities and scrap-metal drives, overseas relief and white-elephant sales. So it was likely that someone as essentially of the common run as she, with few traits that were outstanding or out of the ordinary, should come to be confused, in people's minds, with other names and faces. Only, when she brought home examples of this odd fatality that pursued her, stories of constantly being seen where she wasn't, doing what she hadn't, her husband was impatient, and the silly girls only laughed.

"Just think, Mrs. Everson complimented me today on the fine address I gave, accepting the presidency of the Tuesday Afternoon Club, and I've never attended one of their meetings!"

Carl looked at her warily over the top of a weekly picture magazine but said nothing.

She sat down next to him on the couch, took off her hat, and shook out her new permanent.

"And last week both Adams sisters, the old ladies who run the catering service out of their home, saw me on the street and asked how many was I planning to have in for that buffet supper, and said to give them plenty of notice because they're all tied up at this season. . . . I don't see how they keep in business, they must be getting their orders haywire."

He grunted.

"But the odd part is I *was* thinking of getting someone to sponsor me for the Tuesday Afternoon Club, and the Adams girls must surely have been reading my mind, because I was planning to have them in next time we take on both sides of the family, and was waiting to ask you before making my reservation."

Unable to hold back any longer, the girls rolled to the floor, clutching their sides, and Carl slammed the magazine on the couch and left the room.

So to avoid the ridicule of the young and the disapproval of her husband — when they were alone now he voiced suspicions that in repeating these stories she was exaggerating, milking episodes for all they were worth, adding to the unimportant incident for the sake of a good tale, or even inventing the most extraordinary ones from scratch – to avoid trouble at home, she refrained from carrying back to them the petty encounters as they piled up day by day. She did not tell her husband and children such trivia as being thanked by a recently recuperated club member for a get-well card she'd forgotten to send, of being given kind words by a young husband for a hospital call on his wife and newborn son, whose arrival she hadn't heard about till that moment. Nor mention that the morning after a fund-raising musicale during which all of their family sat in stiff discomfort (none of them having been educated to care much for music), an unknown and elegantly dressed gentleman had approached her on the street, raised his hat, and commended her taste and good musical sense in sponsoring the event.

She kept her silence about all this, but the coincidences and cases of mistaken identity continued to crop up. Hunted down, surrounded, persecuted by false reports about her daily activities; the mistakes ranged from stunning to mildly annoying, from jolting to merely amusing. In one day, she was rumored seen in four nearby towns, she was put on buses, cars, trains, for destinations where she had never set foot, was thanked for extravagant gifts she had not sent, criticized for public statements she had not made, quoted in remarks she had not delivered, credited with opinions she was not capable of formulating. But even so, with much that was puzzling or disturbing in her daily setting, for the woman and her family this was an agreeable, bustling, important, event-laden, and fascinating time – much to plan for, to look forward to, much to do.

But then when things in general are going quite well, something really terrible happens.

One of the young twins is killed in the war, overseas, and

a week after the arrival of the telegram announcing the death, his older sister receives an uncompleted letter written by the soldier, presumably on the day he died, removed from his kit and sent on to her with a decent short note of explanation by another member of his unit.

In this letter, written hours or even minutes before stepping into the ambush that killed him and several other members of their platoon, the boy speaks to his sister of a dream he has had the night before, of being back home with all the members of the family, present and past. The dream, rising with exceptional vividness out of a broken night's sleep, has spurred him to do what he'd had in mind for a long time: write his sister a real letter instead of the brief acknowledgments of the packages and the lively gossip she sends – though he is sure she understands how it's not exactly easy right now to keep up a correspondence. But since he is waiting around anyway to go on patrol, he wants to take a few minutes and put down what he remembers of their life together in that crazy old house (here resurrecting instances of family games and quarrels that she could not in her shocked condition begin to remember); and to say thanks a lot, to her and Carl, for what they'd done for him and Donald. . . .

This unfinished letter, a neutral scrap of paper, showing no sign of the outrage its author had suffered, neither broken nor torn nor desecrated with dirt or blood; written in a familiar handwriting, slightly lopsided as if the writer had been lying flat or bracing himself in a cramped position; the sight of his letter filled the sister with an exultant conviction that the writer must still be alive. The paper was so clean and untouched! It had survived gunfire and the unknown hazards of the battlefield. How could this fragile bit of paper, which could be torn or crumpled up in her fist, survive, and a healthy young man be destroyed?

She sat, holding on to the paper, convinced and radiant, on a dull-colored February morning, until Carl came in, saw what she had, took it from her, then wiped his hands over his face. Although he had cared for the boys, he had not cried when the telegram was delivered nor in the days after. Now she could see his machinist's fingers growing darker and beginning to glisten. She left the letter with him and went up to their bedroom.

But afterward, at the memorial service, when the other twin has obtained leave and has flown in and they are all together, as much of the family as remains, she can barely look them in the face for the shame of it. It seems to her that in dreaming about her so vividly the night before he died, her brother had been calling on her for some assistance that it should have been within her power to give. And since she had presumably found a way to appear before him, why couldn't she also have been able to forewarn and save?

Again and again, she tries to assure herself that it is not so exceptional for someone homesick and frightened to dream his way back to better days. What difference that she was the subject of the dream, any more than the surviving twin, the parents, the older brothers, or even one of the family dogs? Surrounded by the family, the dead boy's friends, the minister, and all the many townspeople she encounters daily, who go up and with subdued faces sympathetically touch her hand, she asks herself what she has done to deserve this latest disgrace and punishment.

So much she had accepted: losing the father, the mother, being thrown too early into too many responsibilities, marrying a man about whom she feels this way then that, raising two scats who even as they stand at her side throughout the ceremony are slyly abstracting their attention, sending their glances wandering through the church, exchanging significant looks, and in general showing their mother how much she will be able to depend on them in the future. Yes, indeed, she had accepted, she had endured, she had bowed her head. But as for this unripe death, which she had been able

neither to anticipate nor prevent, this betrayal of the young
person left in her charge . . . The frivolous strange gift, which
she hates and fears, which seemingly would allow her to appear at any moment before any number of insignificant
strangers, but which for her is useless – a deformity, a curse –
has been involved here, if only by default, and it incriminates
her.

The burden and the blame of this will remain with her for
a long time, although for Carl's sake, for her daughters', the
woman forces herself back into the daily routines. Gradually she picks up where she left off, in the planning and buying and working and keeping up with the groups and
activities. Only, now, when reference is made to her rare
proclivity, when someone alludes to a conversation she knows
has not taken place, when someone mentions catching sight
of her at a church bazaar or supper she has not attended,
or when cheerful wonderment is expressed – "How you do
get around!" – our woman shudders, tries to think of other
things, shuns the speaker, or quietly leaves the group. For
she has begun to suspect that this particular trait might be
connected in some way to disaster.

And there are disasters enough for them all, as the months
drag on. As the war continues and victory comes near, though
not near enough, other men are killed or arrive home in a
pitiful state. She attends memorial services for the brothers,
husbands, sons, of her acquaintances, and becomes familiar with the sermon the minister feels appropriate to deliver
on these occasions. She murmurs comforting words into the
ears of stoical young wives, of bereaved and uncompre-
hending parents. She attends funerals where the body has
been shipped home in a sealed container, and throughout
the ceremony, stares at the flag-draped metal box. At her
brother's funeral, they had not been able even to grieve over
the evidence, and she makes a resolve, which in time

helps pull her strength back, that when this war is over she will make a pilgrimage to the place overseas where he is buried.

4

THEN ONE DAY, finally, wonderfully, the war is over. That much is lifted. So much is changed. But the busy life around them rolls on and gathers momentum, as if in the exultation and relief of those days there is more than ever a need for evening parties, for luncheons, for afternoon visits, for spontaneous get-togethers. Women drop in and out of her house so frequently she almost misses the old quiet days when she must have been lonely. For among the women of her age and situation in this town, she is becoming a local voice, and a leader.

The one meaningful difference in her life – though it is something of a problem too – is that for the first time she has an intimate friend. The friend calls her on the telephone every morning, or she calls the friend. No day can begin without their routine exchange of gossip and confession, and sometimes there is a lengthy evening call as well to sum up and round out what the day has brought in.

The friend is a large, hearty, handsome, expansive, in some ways reckless individual, exuberant and opinionated, who is unhappy – or claims to be unhappy – with her husband. Ruddy and heavy boned, talented and a trifle overpowering. She comes of a family that has been important in their town for two or three generations; she knows everything worth knowing about the personal history and antecedents of everyone in the community, including the most recent arrivals. She is clever, too, with well-developed tastes and interests: music, good cooking, old furniture, identifying birds

23

and plants, needlepoint, advanced theories of child raising. With the friend, a new breadth and intensity enters into the woman's life. Together the two of them scurry off on antique hunts, on shopping expeditions; they exchange dinner parties and experiment with complicated recipes. One misty April day, wearing slickers and galoshes, they hike through a swamp, checking off names from a bird-watcher's handbook, and come back that afternoon mud-plastered and aching, glowing, and shattered with hysterical laughter. Over highballs before dinner, at one house or the other, they exchange morbid and enervating confidences that oscillate like a compass needle before coming to settle on the husbands who fail them, the children who, for all the care with which they have been raised, are growing away, growing into strangers, also beginning to fail them.

And with the new friend, our woman's special condition suddenly flowers into some truly spectacular demonstrations: but the friend is not discommoded in the slightest. "Didn't I tell you I had a sixth sense?" she will ask, dismissing a series of coincidences that would have staggered a less stalwart companion. "Don't mind me – I'm psychic."

Nor are these examples always as petty and innocuous as picking up the phone and being connected without having to dial, because your friend has chosen that second to call, or selecting a book you hope she will enjoy, then coming home to find a copy of it waiting for you. But the sort of thing she would be reluctant to pass along to either Carl or John, Rhoda's narrowly literal and rather small-minded husband.

"But, Rhoda," our woman would breathe her wonderment into the telephone, "of course I'd love to have you along. I was thinking of asking you. But how did you guess I was planning to go to Chicago on Monday, that is, if I can get the appointment?"

"But I'm sure you must have mentioned it, sweetie. You

know me, the original absent-minded marvel. Didn't you say something about it the other day?"

"How could I have, when Carl made the suggestion just last night, before putting out the light? When I told him how dissatisfied I am with Dr. Clint – you know, those loose back teeth he's not doing a thing for – he said, 'Go to the big city then, see a specialist, find out what he can do for you.'"

Well, they made their trip and spent a week at the Palmer House while she consulted her dental specialist, who referred her to another specialist closer to home. And all through it, her friend Rhoda demonstrated remarkable aptitude for – not interference, really, but certainly presence, a relentless presence that never quite released its grip.

Should she slip away for an hour to do some shopping, she would come back to hear Rhoda suggest, "Sweet, I was in Marshall Field's and saw some blouses that would be perfect for your girls. . . ." And Rhoda would describe, down to colors, fabric, and style, the content of the box our woman clutched against her breast.

Should they separate for the day, arranging to meet for tea at the Art Institute, she and Rhoda were bound to bump into one another on at least three different stops, which neither had mentioned or apparently premeditated. Granted that the city, for all its spread, was not so large – that there was a limit to what might be seen or done – still, without either having confided the interest, to meet with joyful ex-clamations under the third-floor rotunda of the Public Library ("I had a sudden mind to see those mosaics"); on the visitor's gallery overlooking the pit at the Board of Trade ("For years I've been curious about corn futures"); or while making a fur-tive and self-conscious inspection of the university our woman's younger daughter had announced as first choice for the coming fall ("Oh, so this where your intellectual Peggy will be trimming the student's lamp!")

Lastly, most mysteriously, encountering one another on

a wind-racked afternoon in one of the city's outer suburbs in a gale so strong neither could hold on to her flower-trimmed hat, staggering up the steps of the Bahai temple –

"Fancy seeing you here, Rhoda!"

"Well, it happens I've always had a longing to visit a midwestern version of the Taj Mahal."

For sheer intensity and immersion, our woman could remember nothing like it, not even during the brief honeymoon span with Carl. Should she wake during the night with an ache or stiffness somewhere, from the other bed would come a jolt and wakening rustle, a light would go on, and, lighting a cigarette, her companion would begin complaining about the identical rheumatic pain or muscle spasm. They began sharing their food reactions. Condiments and seasonings that back home she could tolerate and the other could not were here reversed or extended, so that shortly total confusion set in, and, neither being able to remember which dishes she was sensitive to, they were forced to limit their menus to the plainest and blandest. Not only did they share their physical symptoms, they shared their sleep disturbances and nocturnal disorders. Before the trip, she'd been the one who could not fall asleep unless a room was totally dark, while Rhoda was susceptible to the slightest degree of noise. But now that neither could take the light coming in through the transom or the tiniest sound from outside, a series of restless nights set in.

Calling from bed to bed, apparently they shared their dreams.

"But are you sure, Rhoda, you had a dream that you were back home giving your father a ride on your old porch swing? Because right before the alarm went off, I had this dream where my whole family was sitting crushed up in an enormous rocking chair, having a group portrait snapped, with my father up center naturally, and I got up and gave the chair an enormous *push*."

A week of highly charged intimacies, from which she returned played out, exhausted by the possibility of near-perfect communication. It was as if, during that trip, the two of them had transcended the use of the telephone, of the spoken word entirely. And at one moment she had come near panic. Lying back in the parlor-car on the train ride home, surrounded by the glut of merchandise both had accumulated during the visit, our woman was appalled when Rhoda raised her head with a jerk and murmured, "Are you thrilled or depressed about Emmy's engagement?"

"But how could you know? Not even Carl ... "

"But didn't you tell me? I can *see* you telling me."

"How could I, when she made me swear on the Bible not to mention it until the boy's graduation, not to her own father. If I gave it away, promise, Rhoda, that you won't say a thing!"

It was all right, because in these matters Rhoda was trustworthy: she had an aristocratic sense of honor. But sinking back on the dusty velour seat, the mother felt a revulsion rise toward her seat partner and nervously asked, then am I the one throwing these things out, or is she the one circling in and snatching them? A question to which she received an unsatisfactory answer when the friend, before dropping off again, murmured, "But a divinity student? And will it make you feel safer to have the clergy for a son-in-law?"

After that trip, the woman is unable to throw off a residue of the revulsion and nervousness. Any extended converse with the friend leaves her feeling run-down and drained for days. However this may also be because the friend — for all her enthusiasms and energetic hobbies, the bouncy spirits and infectious laugh — is a woman haunted by multiple fears that spread out around her like invisible rays, or rays that can only be observed under the blackest light: fears of food poisoning, fears of fatal diseases, fears of drastic business losses, fears without name to them, fears of accidents of every shape and description.

An index to the sensitized and overwrought atmosphere our woman has entered is that during the period when she and the friend are still inseparable she is approached in a single afternoon by a couple of breathless acquaintances, the first of whom credits her with a lucky escape from an auto crash when her car has been peacefully laid up in the garage, the second of whom congratulates her for a speedy recovery from a heart attack she has not suffered. All of which she begins to find perverse, dreary, and ultimately too unnerving.

But possibly this is how it has to be with close friends! There seems to be more scope but considerably less breathing-space. A convergence, but also a bondage. Then when you appear to be cutting down on your share of the daily calls, or holding back on a few pieces of information, no matter how trivial or damaging to another party, you stand convicted of disloyalty.

Our woman reluctantly concludes that a friend is not necessarily someone you care for so much as someone who is always there. Eventually she comes to feel about Rhoda as she once felt, briefly, about her own daughters: crowded and pushed in; invaded and badly handled; oppressed and overwhelmed, burdened by a shamed and silent dislike.

When this very close friend is forced by developments in her husband's career to pack up her household and move on to another town, the two thereafter correspond only rarely. For a while there are frequent long-distance calls, but these conversations, for all their revival of a heightened atmosphere and an earlier shared excitement, come to seem cut-off and unnatural. The thrill is gone when you cannot meet again that afternoon to catch up on the latest developments.

The calls taper off, too. From time to time, there is talk, from one or the other, of coming in for a visit, but this never takes place. And when she hears some years later that the friend has died after a devastating illness, our woman does not feel permeated by horror, or washed by pity, or cut down by loss, so much as she suspects that she, herself, is beginning to be used up.

5

THE MOVE TO the new house was strictly on Carl's initiative. By herself, she would never have worked up the interest or the energy. However, long before giving in, she was forced to concede the good sense of her husband's arguments: property values in town were declining, few of their friends lived any longer within its limits, now was the time to jump in and acquire the desirable sites. . . . Not in the direction of her family's old place, off toward the military airfield, but in a spacious settlement accessible to town but countrified enough to allow you to enjoy the style of living that you had spent all these years working to make a reality. Their old house in the country, it seems, had been too far out in the country; the house in town was too much in town; now they would enjoy the best, something in between.

But even after she had begrudgingly thrown up her hands and cried, "All right, go ahead and buy if it means so much to you!" she still found it hard to believe that the projected move would take place. Consequently, she put off planning and was left at the end with decorating problems, awkward tight spaces and problem corners that she had to break her neck finding ways to fill in. Whereas Carl from the start had plunged into the thicket, producing good workable room plans, consulting with the architects – it turned out he'd put down a deposit on a lot while waiting for her to come around – and in general behaving like a school kid who's been handed a yard full of expensive new sporting equipment.

Well, she couldn't blame him, he had worked hard for what he was getting now; but neither could his wife throw herself wholeheartedly into the project, as the man might have preferred. It hurt him, she could see, that she did not spring up and travel eagerly in his footsteps. But he had pushed, he had pushed, and he had had his way. What more could he expect than a worn-down acquiescence?

The difficulty was that although recognizing the sense of the decision, she could not work up any of the feelings required to set into motion all that buying, collecting, fitting in, which tired her beyond belief but which on the other hand elated Carl, infused new blood, gave him a series of interests he hadn't had in years. If she could only lie down and wake up when it was all over! Increasingly, any discussion about their new arrangements ended when the wife (not caring for the expression that came over her husband's face) announced, "I don't care, do as you will, it's all the same to me."

And it was not that, as a good wife, she would deny the attractiveness and meaningfulness of this step for her partner. He had so much more time on his hands now that he was halfway out of the firm and Donald, the surviving twin, was gradually taking over. Why shouldn't Carl enjoy his new leisure by building himself a basement hobby shop, by living close to a country club, by having good-sized grounds to work around in, even a bit of a vegetable garden – let alone a home filled with the latest and most ingenious accessories? Then let him have his way, do as he pleased, only not insist on her approval.

If she'd still had the girls with her, that might have made the difference. But both had attended colleges far away, as had their uncles before them, then married and settled down near their schools; as if propelled by an explosion to the coasts of the country, leaving the parents sinking into a kind of cavity in the middle. But the father had chosen to turn his cavity into a permanent wood-working shop or well-tended putting green, while the mother was left to spend her time supervising a too comfortable house, driving the maid back and forth from the station, and investing hours in resting her manicured hands in her lap in front of the latest-model television screen.

Her main grievance against their new house was that it was too comfortable, too convenient. There were not enough of those malfunctioning, lovable eccentricities she now looked back on with nostalgia in the previous home which they had faithlessly abandoned, but which they had been grateful enough to move into, during the days of shortages and war-time scarcities. If there had been just one electric outlet that didn't work! But Carl had planned the place down to the last wall socket and plastic counter and had done a spectacular job of it, their friends, even the architect, agreed. Whatever went wrong nowadays couldn't be blamed on the house but on the human beings inside the house. Or on something even more difficult to pin down.

For if you ever thought that you could escape from old afflictions simply by packing up and moving to a new address, you were rather wrong. You hardly needed the first idiotic greeting you were blessed with, shouted out by a furiously pedaling delivery boy, who seemed to be defective, who leaned forward from his dangerously careering grocery cart and adenoidally warbled, "Welcome back!" at your first step into the parking lot of the new shopping center.

In the days following, the greeting was repeated at the local gas station, at the hardware mart, by a Fuller Brush salesman who knocked at their door, by the locker-room attendant at the little lakeshore country club, at the beauty parlor. From all of them, she heard variations of "Nice to see you again," "How've you been?" "Where keeping yourself late-ly?" and "Good to have you back." The repetition was sicken-ing. As far as these people were concerned, she might never have been away. From their point of view, she wondered whether she had even returned.

She made no attempt to track down the identity of her presumed model here, knowing from experience that this sort of search would only run her off a blind cliff; but she could not help wondering at times what her predecessor in the area had been like. Was she, this unknown woman, still alive? Did she live nearby? Had she gone away for a time, then returned, coincidentally with the arrival of our woman on the scene? Would the two of them ever pass unknowingly on a street or sit waiting in adjacent cars at a long traffic signal, or shoulder to shoulder in a local store send toward the other a distant, not unfriendly smile? Had this meeting already taken place, many times over? Were the two in frequent contact? In her new isolation and in the absence of more stimulating concerns, the woman found herself at times longing for the approach of this long-avoided, long-pursued, overly familiar other.

Meanwhile, she did, she really did her best to put up with Carl as he went about improving his leisure hours. The projects that the man had apparently been storing up all his life! It was as if the belt on a great piece of machinery had broken, or come loose – he simply did not know which way to lash out first. Hobbies? These were not diversions he had saddled himself with: they were unassailable moral obligations. And the very least would have taken a healthy lifetime to fulfill.

While the wife went about her shrunken responsibilities, ferrying her maid to the station, pushing a cart through the spanking new supermarket, running off to garden-club lectures and memory-improvement courses at the homes of nearby acquaintances whom she could not work up very much taste for, the husband settled down in his chair for hours of zesty catalogue reading. How many improvements could one home support? And how many interests could one man profitably follow? But each time she came down to his knotty-pine-paneled den, to rest her well-kept hands in her lap and sit for a minute helplessly staring at the brown walls with their lighter whorls that inspected her like chilly eyes looking for evidences of fraud, she would find Carl working up still another new interest from the pages of those catalogues: on boating (starting by building your own craft), large-scale landscape gardening, Japanese rock gardening, tree stunting, putting up and maintaining your own greenhouses. He had manuals on stocking tanks with tropical fish, on building kennels and dog runs, on breeding collies, and he was even reading up on raising Black Angus cattle, although, thank God, their grounds were much too small.

On his bedside table, Carl kept a pile of catalogues from L. L. Bean, giving special attention to the winter-sports equipment and the illustrations of various types of fishing gear and weaponry – not that he'd had any previous interest in outdoor sports except golf, and had never hunted or fished for anything in his life. Judging from the material he sent away for, the man was forever poised on the edge of starting a collection of rare shells, semiprecious gems, Colonial pewter, scale-model reproductions of locomotives and sailing ships. He was going to put together a grandfather clock from a kit. He was absorbed in diagrams for installing a sound-system that would have outlets into all the rooms in the house, including the bathrooms. So far the one completed achievement was setting up a pool table down in the game room, where he spent hours contentedly tapping small balls home to their pockets.

From a New York store that specialized in advanced kitchen equipment, Carl was forever sending away for machines that could extract in a few seconds' time the juices from an entire gardenful of vegetables; machines that would chop, dice, pulverize, purée, blend, whip, shake, or otherwise make the original foodstuffs unrecognizable. By now he had an extensive variety of objects for pulling corks from bottles, charging clear water with bubbles, turning meat on complicated spits, keeping it at the proper temperature until it could be served up on electrically warmed plates. Some of the machinery he introduced into the household was so specialized that neither the housewife nor her maid had mastered its operation. Nothing like it – the maid reported from her point of entrée into other kitchens – was to be found in the entire community. On occasion, she took home under her arm as gifts implements which had been supplanted by the arrival of a new generation of machines – castoffs so up-to-date that they had yet to make their appearance on the shelves of the local merchants.

Even so, this newest home, with its inventive comforts and remarkable contrivances, is in some ways a disappointment. For all the attention it demands and constantly receives, nothing in the house works exactly as it should. Or rather, from things working so very well, they begin to work a little too well. In their zeal to be cooperative, the various parts start acting a little independently, almost out of control. Windows slide up and down at the brush of a hand, the drapes move too easily on their rods. You are constantly surprised by something going "Whooosh" or "Whirrr." The ventilating system overresponds to their intentions: too hot in winter, in summer it is too cool. Everything in the house seems to participate a little too animatedly, a little too alertly, as if each piece of equipment is constantly standing at attention, ready to receive orders.

When the woman goes up to bed at night, it disturbs her to think of that shiny and pastel kitchen given over to itself, freed of the interlopers who come in to stir and agitate and leave grease spots and sordid fingerprints behind. At night, restless, unable to sleep, she is reluctant to go down and open the refrigerator for a glass of milk, to take the cover off the toaster and put in a slice of bread, fearing her entrance might be resented as an intrusion by those powerful implements dedicated to their intense, narrow functions.

It is as if, walking in there alone in the middle of the night and watching the room spring into being under the fluorescent fixture, she is stepping into some workshop kept up a little too immaculately to be intended in good faith; like coming upon a counterful of surgical tools where you least expect them, or a display of instruments of torture. . . . Or possibly she is squeamish about intruding on their dreams? At night, after she has wiped off the last traces of use and has muffled these objects in their plastic coverings, do *they* settle down to a long dream of her? Has she become incorporated into their visions, as well as into all those others'? It is as if she can own nothing; but everything she touches, everything she looks at, can claim and carry away a piece of her.

The next morning, after a bad night, half-remembering some wild ideas, the woman sits in a kitchen chair watching her maid using copper polish on the panoply of equipment that lends distinction to their home. It is true that in the morning it all looks a good deal less sinister. The maid stops to ask a question or make a remark, the woman answers, then critically examines the chipped manicure she is about to have renewed within the hour. After so many years, it is her first winter back in the country. Where she sits, ready to go into the garage to warm up her car for the trip, she sees white fields, lines of fuzzy brown shrubbery, emphatic upright sweeps of evergreen. The driveways and paths of their house have been cleared by Carl, although she has scolded him for the exertion. Just a minute more she puts off leaving, and bends over to add her breath to the steamed-up glass. How ridiculous, she thinks, it would be to install a greenhouse here, when she herself has become like a plant kept from the weather, snug under glass.

6

THAT SEASON BECOMES another season, other seasons follow; a year passes, or two. The man and wife are older, more tied to their wonderful house, more thrown in on one another for company, less pleased with being so much together. Small difficulties are beginning to fill out. For one, she simply cannot get used to having a man underfoot, who out of his own lack of occupation and restless nature keeps interfering with her few established routines. It was far worse in winter, when he would hang around the kitchen, making disruptive suggestions about menus and laying a hand on the projects she had been saving up for herself. The morning they got into a struggle over who would polish the sterling, she turned against him completely and said, "Carl, maybe you just weren't cut out for the leisure life. Maybe you ought to find something better to keep you!"

But at his age what new thing was there for him? The man had grown childish, she decided, watching him give the little job the same concentration he once devoted to grinding intricate machine parts. No longer a factory boss, he had taken on the less taxing work of bossing her and the maid.

Then he had changed, to the point where he was requesting her opinion on matters he had never found worth his while discussing at home. Politics: did she have an idea where this country was headed, how far and how fast? Inflation: did she realize how little yield there was on their investments? Sports: some wives took an interest, but she never had, so what was the sense of pumping her head full of scores and percentages? The man was entitled to all the hours he cared to invest sitting at the television watching other men pitch balls or knock one another around, but why drag her in?

When he started reading aloud the records of this team's progress or that player's good season, she had to cry, "Stop, Carl! You're only making me dizzy." Calling for attention, he was consulting her about his wardrobe: should he try thermal underwear? What did she think of the latest trend in neckties? Well, he had never let any of the women in his household interfere with his clothing, not even when the girls begged him to invest in a tuxedo instead of wearing the same dark suit to weddings, banquets, and business meetings – so if that was how he wanted it, let him carry on.

Sorting out his basement den, Carl came on some movie reels taken at their last big reunion, when both girls, the husbands, and the youngsters all came to celebrate the housewarming. Foresaking baseball and football, he took to running them through his projector in the evenings, absorbed as if he had never before seen any of these figures, captured at unlikely angles, weirdly out of proportion, in colors not quite known on this planet. Enormous babies toddled or danced up garden walks. They stooped to close plump fists around stalks of iris colored so intensely violet as to look poisonous. Two young women darted after these children or leaned back, laughing at some fiendish joke, on lounge chairs set down on improbably green lawns.

Their husbands stood seriously contemplating red-purple meats being grilled on outdoor barbeques, as if they were magicians, or surgeons called in for consultation on some diseased organ. The chefs' hats the boys sported were of a whiteness verging on blue. And here – at this moment Carl always reached out in the darkened room and pulled her hand – they stood, the two of them, grim and formidable, or, if you like, handsome and dignified, posing in uneasy ownership on their terrace steps. Behind them the house loomed up, too big, a pinkish off-brown, like a real mansion, an institution.

Each of these nightly showings left the woman feeling more remote and dissatisfied. Who were those small children, known only from occasional visits or little anecdotes passed along in letters? Who were these young women with too bright hair and carnivorous smiles that seemed to lunge through the roll-down movie screen? Lately, Carl had taken to bringing out the old photo albums in the evenings as well, lingering over Brownie snaps of tiny girls on a beach with sun pinafores and sand shovels, holding a young mother by the hand as she stands in an out-of-date bathing suit, squinting into the sun; snapshots of small girls on tricycles, big girls in graduation pictures, young ladies in long dresses waiting to be picked up for a prom.

Leafing through an album, her stiffened fingers with their polished tips hesitating above the glossy rectangles, the woman is struck by a longing for someone not included. Weary of turning pages, she pushes the book away. Evading her husband's eyes, she stares into the corners of the room, in search of someone familiar and elusive. Someone she has known and not known, who has anticipated and run ahead of her, stood apart yet followed her, who has pursued and hidden from her all her life. Our woman has begun to suspect that this unknown person might be the only friend she will ever have.

Weeks spin out into months, months loosen into this year or another. Things happen, or they don't happen. Life pushes on – but with this difference, that Carl has come to believe in her.

He accepts what for so long he has been repudiating, she is vindicated in what she has been telling him all this while, he will no longer be able to express doubts – but she is confirmed by way of the worst thing that happens to her in her life.

But even before that afternoon by the lake that forced their lives into a different pattern, small changes had begun to show. At her side, now scolding and nagging, now pulling and appealing, Carl becomes a witness. And as recognition dawns, he makes a last stab to fend it off by blaming *her.*

"Why couldn't you talk to Mrs. Vigler when you were at the club today?" Carl came in on a spring afternoon, remarkably irritated. "I ran into her, just now, and she seems upset. Naturally, she told me she was worried about you. But you might have managed a few words. Remember Dr. Vigler came in the middle of the night when I had my back pains?"

"Did Mrs. Vigler tell you I didn't see her at the club? Today?"

"You couldn't have missed seeing her."

"But Carl, I wasn't at the club today!"

Carl shook his head, incredulous and impatient. "You're so sure about that?"

"I was absolutely nowhere in the vicinity!"

"Well, to hear her say it, you sat at the next table at lunch, and when she leaned over to ask how I was doing, you pushed your table back and made a run for it. She wondered if you'd been taken with something, you got out so fast."

"But, Carl." She seized his jacket. "You've got to believe I was nowhere near the club today. After you left, I drove over to the stationery store to pick out a card to send with Emmy's birthday check. Then I decided to stop off at the garage to have Sam check my brakes – apparently they don't need tightening. I came right back and had lunch here." She pointed to the rack, where dishes were draining.

Carl was breathing hard. "She seemed dead certain. How do you explain it? Well," he decided, "she must have made a mistake. We better have the Viglers over some evening. I wonder who that other fool woman was."

A short time afterward, a salesman came to their house,

one of a crew working up and down the neighborhood. Carl closed the door on him and walked back toward the kitchen, working up a temper.

"Why did you tell that young fellow to come back for my signature? You know I never buy anything from door-to-door solicitors."

"A salesman? What selling?"

"I don't know, some kind of encyclopedia, set of reference books. I didn't stop to listen. But I wonder that you'd waste his time, telling him to return."

"But I never did!"

"You sure it hasn't slipped your mind, a little detail?" This time he tried sarcasm, bluff condescension.

"Nobody came to the door while you were out today," she assured him gently. "If anybody had, I'd have done the same as you – sent him away."

"But I don't see how he could have made the mistake." Carl refused to look at her. "He acted so damned sure of himself. He knew I drove in to the factory this morning! He said the lady asked him to come back and take it up with the man of the house."

"Yes, and I bet he's been saying that up and down the neighborhood. Well, possibly he's confusing us with another family. The Arnolds – you know Curt goes off every day. Or the Terrys – Lila Terry is always looking for new ways to improve her mind."

"It was very strange," Carl finished. "Damn these salesmen. They're always thinking up ways to make trouble."

It was unfortunate that Carl happened to answer the telephone, the day Lila Terry rang up and breathlessly demanded to hear how things were going. This time it seemed Bill Terry had picked up a story from some source (by the time Carl hung up he was too muddled to patch together details) that our woman had been savagely beaten by a prowler that morning and carried off for an emergency operation.

"Operation?" She could hear Carl, trying to hold down his voice. "What do they mean, an operation? Nobody been prowling around here, and my wife's still in one piece, thank you. She's in the kitchen right now, talking with the maid."

Carl came back into the room flushed with outrage. Never had he lived in such a rumor-mongering community. It was driving him out of his mind. In a long winter, the women were apparently ready to go to any lengths to whip up some excitement.

"But Carl, didn't you say it was a man told Bill ... "

"What difference does it make? Why does your name have to enter in?"

"I don't think they meant anything unfriendly."

"Well, why don't they find another target? Why don't they leave you out of it?" Carl's face was filmed over by a curtain of indecision and disbelief; the skin was turning gray. "Why does the whole world have to keep making these mistakes about *you*?"

Anger turned the tables on disbelief, his color flooded back. "Now who," he wanted to know, "could have been going around spreading that kind of stupid misinformation?"

The maid, folding her work clothes away in a shopping bag, looked up, after years of working in other people's houses prepared for anything. Back from driving her to the station, Carl had an inspiration: "What say from now on we take care of the place ourselves? There's little enough to do. In my opinion, we've both been getting too soft."

"As you like," his wife agreed. After all, she had seen it coming! But if Carl hoped to be let off with the explanation that it was the maid's fault — gossiping, spreading false stories — if he had contrived to ransom his domestic peace by removing a foreign body from his household; if he hoped to buy back harmony and defeat the forces lined up against him by the simple sacrifice of the maid's services, then he was hoping to buy back much too cheaply. In the week after the maid had been given notice and after Carl had taken over the heavy work himself, scrubbing, waxing, weekend marketing, he came home with a number of very puzzling additions.

The owner of the dry cleaner's had asked in an insinuating voice, "Things all right at your house?" When Carl snapped back that everything was fine, he had looked dubious.

"I see the wife's out of town" was a frequent remark. Often it became more specific:

"I see your wife went off to visit your son."

"That's news to me. We have no son."

"Daughter, was it? I saw her checking in at the airport yesterday, when I flew back from the Coast."

"My wife, thank you, is still at home with me," Carl would cry out, "or was, up to half an hour ago!"

Letters would arrive from stores where she did not have an account: "Dear Madame, Our records show we have not had occasion to serve you for the past three years. If we can be of assistance and if you would care to view our new spring collection . . ."

"Double damn!" Carl would exclaim, before disposing of the letter. "Don't they know when to let up?"

And the telephone continued to pursue them, even after Carl had stopped answering it, the way he was letting mail pile up for days under their door-slot. The telephone bell became a signal for man and wife to jump up and put on furtive expressions. A summons that the woman herself would reluctantly respond to, after the ringing had gone on so long as to make them feel cornered. And when she hung up, Carl could recognize in her face some new intrusion.

"What was it this time?"

"Nothing," she assured him. "Just Marian Long. She wondered why she hadn't seen us lately. Everybody was at the Leary's anniversary party Sunday. I told her our invitation must have got lost in the mail."

"I don't suppose she had some dumb explanation?"

"Well, I'm supposed to have had this terrible quarrel with Mrs. Leary because our dog nipped one of the Leary grandchildren. They're saying I refused to take him in for observation."

"What dog?" Carl shouted. His hands were shaking. "Raffles died eight years ago."

"I told Marian there was nothing to it. But couldn't very well say, could I, that we hadn't opened the Leary invitation until the party was over?"

As weeks passed and as that winter neared its end, Carl stayed firmly attached to the house and grounds; it became impossible to pry him loose. When there were errands to do, he maneuvered it so they went off together, like, she thought contemptuously, a couple of old nuns. Apparently he did not trust her out of his sight. On the way home from these expeditions, Carl complained in a petulant voice of the shabby treatment they were being given in the community – the way one person looked at them, the next had spoken. These days he carried around a puzzled look, a shamefaced, blinking mannerism, a hangdog way of responding to every little overture, that made her want to laugh. Couldn't he profit by his own advice and pretend these things had never happened? What difference to him, that she was seen by eyewitnesses enjoying herself down in the Florida sun, or was reported feuding with the whole lot of their neighbors?

"For heaven's sake!" she would lash out, near the breaking-point, "let the others talk as they please, what difference to us?"

This quality of hers, special tendency, or plain string of bad luck – nowadays the man rode and worried it to the point where the wife was forced to downgrade and make light of what her partner was taking much more seriously. Well, it may have been new to him, but she was an old hand at the game. She had developed muscle in the struggle. And now that his eyes were beginning to open, it seemed doubly

43

unfair that she should have to offer comfort and consolation to her husband, in his present state of distress.

Seeing Carl stoop with a groan and pick up the local paper, hearing the half-joking remark "Let's see what new lies they've cooked up this week!" and watching him lick a finger and jauntily turn pages, the woman reminded herself how often now she absolutely could not stand him.

Eventually, the trouble in their lives turns and twists until even her brother, Donald, gets tangled up in its webbing.

"We decided to drive out and see how you folks were getting along," Donald explained, after Carl had grudgingly gone to the front door.

"You sure are hard people to reach!" Donald's wife commented.

"We haven't been in much." Carl backed into the room, blinking his light lashes, but the woman sat fast in her corner, anticipating some new disgrace.

"More power to you," her sister-in-law remarked. She tossed a new mink coat over the back of her chair, and wouldn't let Carl hang it up. They were stopping only a minute, she explained.

"Just to see how you folks were doing," Donald repeated, rubbing his knuckles. Had his twin survived, the woman asked, would he have blown on his hands that same way to flex and warm them? Would he have developed that particular ritual tapping of the fingers?

"I had them call you three times from the factory last week about business," he said, "but they couldn't get an answer. We haven't been able to reach you evenings, either."

"Well, it does happen we've been out a lot." Carl slumped farther into his chair.

"You don't have to tell me *you've* been circulating" — Donald's wife turned to her. "And you must be getting pretty nearsighted too. Have you had your eyes checked lately? You sat two pews in front of me at Dawson's funeral, and I couldn't catch your attention on the way out, though I pretty darn near tripped you the next day, when you walked right by my table at the antique fair."

"Antique fair?" Carl echoed.

"But I bet you were purposely avoiding me, admit it, Monday at the fur sale." She stroked the glossy pelt. "What's the matter, Carl? Are you getting mean in your old age? Does your wife have to sneak out and try on minks all by herself and pretend no one she knows is watching? Go out and buy her a new coat. It will do wonders for your circulation."

"It must have been my double you saw those times," the woman said evenly. "I haven't been able to get away to do any shopping in weeks. I could use some new clothes, too — that's a very pretty coat you have there — but I'm not supposed to leave *him*, and who cares to drag a man around from store to store?"

Soon after, Carl, looking foolish and shamed, walked their visitors to the door. The woman sat on, staring into the corner. Carl went up to bed by himself, his wife remained a good part of the night downstairs, watching her corner. What she had done, she was justified in doing, but she would have pitied him if she'd had that much in her.

7

WHEN SHE DROVE up late and saw the state police parked across their driveway, immediately she knew she should not have stayed away so long. But it had been such a relief, getting off alone for a change, not having to make way for anyone's schedule, listen to anyone's grumbling. His back was giving him trouble, he couldn't stand being shaken up in a car. Treat yourself to a rest, she advised, stay home.

After finishing some shopping, she rolled the windows down and went for a spin, welcoming the breezes, rough and gusty at times, that opened the pores of her face and made a mess of her hair. It had been a reawakening – the trees leafed out, the roadside shoulders green and downy, dogwood spilling down the embankments, the heavy car handling like silk, traffic well spaced and moving freely.

For a couple of hours she just drove, following one road, then another, getting into unfamiliar territory and having to pull up and check a road map. Cruising well above the speed limit, she'd indulged the hope that the winter's piled-up troubles might be passed as easily as the scenery, that they might melt away with the last patches of ice on their driveway. Then to come back and find a state trooper blocking her entrance.

When she leaned from the window, waved, and honked, the trooper stared at her and said to Carl, "Is that by any chance your wife?" At his wordless nod, the man took off his hat, and shook Carl's hand in pantomime congratulation. He seemed inexplicably pleased, but Carl, at the sight of her, looked frightened and grim. He was standing there blurry and receding into the bright light, like a television picture in need of contrast tuning: hair white, face white, wearing washed-out whitish chinos.

"Sorry to have troubled you," the trooper said. His face was a glowing tan, his uniform was green, his boots were glossy. "Believe me, mister, it's not our favorite type of case. Well, back to headquarters."

He got into his car, and she had to back up to let him out. By the time she pulled in, picked her things off the seat, and slammed the door, he was gone. "What's wrong? What did he want?" she cried, but Carl had disappeared already inside the house.

He refused to look her in the face when she entered. She had to drag the story out word by word. There had been a bad accident – that she got right away. To an older woman.

Down by the lake. Near the country club. A drowning, the trooper said.

"Was it anyone we know? Why did the police come here?" Carl looked at her.

"But, Carl, what's wrong then?"

"There seemed to be a little error in naming the victim."

"Oh, Carl – no!"

"I was positive it couldn't be you. I tell you I wasn't at all worried. I knew you'd never get into a sailboat by yourself, when I can't get you out in one with me."

"Why, Carl, neither of us has been near that club in months. Why should anyone imagine now . . ."

The mix-up, as it came out, was entirely the fault of the high-school boy who had the job of handling the boats in the afternoons. In the panic and excitement of the moment, he'd named her as the woman who'd gone out in the unlucky boat. The club had been nearly deserted at that hour, anyway, and no one there had been in a position to correct or contradict him. In fact, he'd seemed so sure of himself that, rather than trace the deceased woman through her license plates, the trooper had driven straight to Carl to break the news and take him to identify the body. He'd been trying to persuade Carl to come with him when she drove up.

"Oh, Carl, what a terrible thing to happen. On that beautiful lake. *How?* And who was it, then?"

"I don't know," Carl said. But his look was more accusing than relieved.

And well he might accuse, because from then on they entered a modified state of siege. The boy had also given her name to a reporter from the local weekly, and the reporter, rushing to make an issue, had printed the story without checking his facts. Her picture, from a group photo in their files, appeared on page two that week, with a full account of the tragedy.

As soon as the paper was out, Carl phoned both daughters,

who were puzzled, then alarmed, then relieved. There was nervous laughter and mutual congratulations – when all the while the presumed victim had been nowhere near the scene of the event. After Carl had called up the editor and given him holy hell, the editor sent a sympathetic reporter, who promised to run a corrected story and an apology the following week. But meanwhile what was to stop the cars driving up, the telephone besieging them at all hours? How could you even blame the callers?

It almost killed her to think of her name passed like bad currency from mouth to mouth. How was it possible they possessed, she and Carl, such a contingent of well-wishers in the immediate locality? And that each person would find it necessary to repeat, with little variation, pleasure at the way things had turned out; as if everyone took joy in consigning the other woman to her doom!

She would have nothing to do with those eager scavengers. When the phone rang now, when the curious drove to their door, she walked into the next room and Carl was left to explain she was suffering shock.

For two things she blamed herself as near criminally culpable. It had been foolhardy to expect any improvement in the situation, and it had been inviting disaster to stay out so long, enjoying herself, the afternoon of the tragedy. Had she stayed where she belonged, in the long run she would have done less harm.

In the future, the woman vowed, she would remain quietly inside where no one could see her – safe from these dangerous invocations of her name, shielded from those presses out there that stamp out an unending series of replications. . . . And after some days of keeping to the house, resisting the impulse to step outdoors, although he weather had turned hot and the garden badly needs weeding, the phone calls did begin to taper off, and she stopped wincing at the noise of wheels turning up their drive.

After that, she gave up coming downstairs entirely, letting Carl handle things below and throw his meals together as best he could. Having the run of the place must have been agreeable to him, however, because from that time on he made his bed in his den, coming up during the day carrying the tea or toast or boiled egg that was all, in her present condition, she could swallow.

As she sat on the unmade bed or hunched in a bedside chair or stared into the dusty dressing-table mirror, the woman did not think of her daughters, or of Carl, or of the well-meaning soul who had sent flowers. She did no thinking at all. Only, in her own home, in her own room, being careful to move around as little as possible, she senses she will be less likely to set into motion those shock waves that fan out from her body and inflict damage and hurt on others. So, after another day or two, she also stops getting out of bed.

Waking early, she lay in her twin bed, across from the empty one, watching the early-summer sun touch up the ivory wallpaper to match the dull-rose lining of the drapes. By noon the room glowed like a rosy pearl, but inside it she lay cold and white and washed up as a shell. If she thought about anything these days, she might wonder about the dead woman.

The victim's photo, printed with the full story in the next issue of the paper, had given nothing away. A studio portrait, blandly resisting interpretation, of a considerably older woman, wearing glasses with tiny rhinestones set in the frame, the hair restrained by an invisible hairnet and touched up with a bluish rinse . . . a woman from somewhere else, a visitor, a total stranger. The mother of one of the local younger families, recently settled in. Nobody seemed to know any more than that about them.

To say the least she had been, the dead woman, a person of remarkably poor judgment! Why had she chosen a squally day to go for a sail without a life jacket in a boat that she obviously lacked the skill to handle? Under the circumstances, why did she take along a small child? Then after the boat had tipped and help was on the way, why had she let go? Was her grip so weak? Did she panic so easily? Couldn't she have held on for the sake of the grandchild? According to the paper, the little boy's body had not been recovered until the next day. They had had to dive for it, repeatedly, to the bottom of the lake.

Out in a tiny boat, with a squall coming up, with a child who is frightened and for that reason misbehaving. Not worried at first or not realizing how worried, but gallantly trying to cope. Having to comfort, then admonish, then hold down a frantic child: "Now sit quiet, Timmy, and behave yourself. Wait till your father hears about this!" A child who in a yearning toward shore leans too far over and falls in. Reaching out to pull him up, and tipping the boat; now both are in the water. One arm around a struggling child, she tries to hold on to a slippery keel . . .

Carl runs up the stairs, white-faced, one hand on his chest. "Why are you yelling like that? Are you sick? Do you want me to call a doctor?"

"No, don't, I won't see a doctor. All I need is to be left in peace. Please go away, Carl. Let me get some rest."

The worst is that as she lies there, the drowned woman keeps getting confused in her mind with a saying, dredged up from some forgotten source: *The devil finds work for idle hands.* That the devil manages to find occupation for idle hands was a rule our woman had never any reason before to doubt. Then why should the proposition, each time she thinks of it, bring tears to her eyes, plus an elated sense of discovery: as if the words are charged with a blissful meaning reserved for her alone?

The blissful sensation is interrupted by the image of the retarded delivery boy who had accosted her in the shopping-center parking lot with the foul greeting "Welcome back!" the day of her arrival. At the time, it was the last thing you would have expected. Whoever he was, this creature, he was hardly an appropriate introduction to such a pleasant retreat, where there are so many large houses set back on well-tended lawns, with flagstone terraces and ornamental trees and barbeque pits, all, and tennis courts, some, and swimming-pools, others, and riding horses, a few. With speedboats and show-place gardens and greenhouses.

This creature resembled nobody to be seen in the vicinity. His parents may have been comfortable or well-off people, but he was deformed or in some way incomplete, sheep-faced, adenoidal. You could surmise at a glance that he was filthy to an extreme. His nose was running unattended, his hair hung over his forehead like some wayward animal covering, his spade-like teeth were planted in long pale gums, the light in his eye would not bear definition. And he was clearly enjoying himself – having a glorious time driving his cart, yodeling and swerving, in and out among the standing, expensive cars. She remembered walking around and making a careful check of hers before getting back in.

"What's this?"

Carl, coming up with a bowl of creamed soup, scattered down on her bed a flutter of cathedrals, Alps, grim castles, sunny squares surrounded by statues.

"I've been to see a travel agent," he told her. "I've been thinking it might be good to get away for a while, see the world. There's no reason against going. Is there?"

"You're asking me to take a trip?" She made a gesture toward the bed where she lay.

Not right this second, Carl assured her; but she'd be feeling better eventually, wouldn't she? They could start planning now for a trip this fall.

"Why not?" he demanded with some of his old authority. Not stopping for an answer, he went on to quote what he'd apparently learned from the agent and the brochures concerning the benefits of seeing Europe in the fall, away from the rush of travelers. He enthusiastically named places she'd had no idea he had any previous desire to view. He spoke knowingly of bargain shopping and rates of exchange and beneficial climate conditions. He projected an extended, mellow, autumn ramble; the voyage was magically compacted into those glossy brochures that lay spilled over her bedsheet. And the best, he told her, was that everything could be arranged through that fellow in the travel bureau. All that would be required of her was to get up out of bed, and move.

"And if you still want" – Carl hesitated – "we could combine it with a visit to that place over there where your brother's buried. I thought you always had that in mind."

"Well, yes, it's an idea." And the woman reached out and touched his hand.

When she is a little stronger, she will have to explain to him that it will not do. She had no interest in seeing other parts of the world, and why go to all that trouble to visit a grave? Besides, in a manner of speaking, she has had the duplicate of the dead brother living quite near her all these years. Had he survived, he would doubtless have turned out to be the same sort of person as his twin, with the same collection of mannerisms, tastes, jokes, opinions, minor faults. By now the boy in the ground is hardly more dead to her than the man who has remained above ground. For such a man, she tells herself, she would not go all the way across the ocean.

"All right, I'll think about it." She puts her husband off, waiting for this latest enthusiasm to pass.

No, she would not chase off to foreign places – Florence, Frankfurt, London – because she suspects as soon as she sets foot in any of their streets, a deranged delivery boy will come bicycling toward her, chortling the equivalent of "Welcome back!" in his baffling foreign tongue. By now she hardly doubts that a demented delivery boy, cracking his gum and pedaling furiously, will lean from his vehicle and carol "Welcome back!" on her arrival in hell.

8

ALERTED BY SOME puzzling comments in notes from her Uncle Donald, spurred on by the elusive tone of her father's letters, and the fact that her mother has stopped writing entirely, limiting herself to a few words scrawled at the bottom of his, the younger daughter arrives unannounced on a visit and is shocked to discover that her mother has not been out of the house all summer.

She is also distressed to see her father noticeably aged since the last time she saw him, shrunken, unsteady in manner, hesitant about expressing himself, with a look on his face she can only construe as embarrassed guilt. To her questions, he gives unsatisfactory replies: people had been bothering her mother, to some extent. There was trouble, unspecified, with the neighbors. As evidence he offers an annoying collection of conjectures and suppositions that she impatiently brushes off. The one solid fact in this confusion is a scandal growing out of the unfortunate incident that occurred down by the lake, months ago, which seemed to have subjected her mother to unwelcome attention in the local press.

"What does it matter what gets printed in that rag?" the daughter cries. "You mean to say, anyone takes it seriously? Besides, Dad, that was months ago. She hasn't gotten over it yet?"

Invited out for a ride, the mother accepts, without spirit. Coaxed to step outside and see what needs to be done, she simply finds a garden chair and sits. Taken out to a restaurant, she throws on a few badly matching garments and endures the meal; urged to invite a few friends over for an evening, she refuses. She also refuses to take any interest in her home, to reclaim her neglected surroundings – to have someone in to take up the rugs and put on summer slipcovers – to buy groceries, or to cook.

. "You mean to say it's been going on like this, the whole time?" the daughter repeats. "You're not eating, she hasn't been eating, really, Dad, you're going to have to take in a housekeeper, at least till we get her back on her on her feet!"

The woman reacts to this suggestion with alarm and contempt, but she is prevailed upon to let a doctor examine her, to prescribe some medicine or revitalizing tonic. The doctor, after the examination and after a talk with his patient, suggests another doctor; this doctor suggests still another, and so it is that the man and his wife are driving home one autumn day, after nearly a week spent in another city, where the woman has been undergoing tests and observation at a special clinic. As they drive along, they have a good laugh over the stupidity of the doctors.

The woman is wearing a tweed suit that echoes the burnished golds and oak-leaf russets that spill down the ravines on both sides of the road. Her husband has on a silver-buttoned blazer that matches the color of his car. They are climatically shut in, protected from drafts and the fumes and odors of the highway. The brilliant scenery passes very, very swiftly.

He reaches over and gives his wife's thigh a homey squeeze. She refrains from comment on how fast he is driving. He chuckles and offers her a cigarette.

"Well!"

"Well?"

"Well," he says, "I think we're going to make it."

The woman leans back reflectively, holding the cigarette between the third and fourth fingers of her freckled, birdlike hand. She has pulled herself up for the journey and is pleased with the way she looks. She is also satisfied with how she has handled herself with the doctors.

"Yes," Carl repeats, "I guess we'll make it."

He gives her a tap, this time on the shoulder, and they share another laugh over the simple-mindedness of the professional men.

Now how, she thinks, just how could she be sick? Sick people heard voices, but hers was the voice that was heard. Sick people were haunted by visions and delusions, but she was the agent that was seen. Far and wide. Impossible to explain (though she had tried) that chunks of her were simply detaching themselves and floating off, going their independent courses as others, the world, seemingly would have it. Some fixative that normally holds lives together was prevented from working in her case. Whatever it was, for her it no longer applied.

Possibly, she thinks, if Carl had been clever enough, he might have hit on a formula for keeping her intact. Nowadays, of course, she realizes the man is as powerless as she.

"Hold tight, old girl," Carl tells her with less conviction. "Something tells me we're going to get there."

Really, she asks, staring at Carl's hands on the wheel, that are pudgy but reveal past strengths, how could those doctors be so foolish as to suggest he stay and share in his wife's treatment -- when neither of them is sick?

Time staggers forward; event lurches toward succeeding event; fall becomes winter, winter collapses into spring, and the older daughter arrives on a visit, bringing her husband, an Episcopalian clergyman, a jolly bald boy dressed in sports clothes, smelling of expensive men's cologne.

He seems pleased and amazed, simultaneously, by everything he encounters around him. His mother-in-law is dissatisfied with her new housekeeper? Exceptional! Neither of them can stand the housekeeper's cooking, but the wife lacks the zest and appetite to function on her own? Extraordinary! His interest and concern reaches out and embraces the trivia of their domestic existence, and is arrested by the harmless little belief, that his father-in-law is now jokingly permitted to refer to even in the old woman's presence; the fixed idea she has carried about all these years like an exotic pet or hobby.

The doctors' warnings, in retrospect, have sufficiently impressed Carl that his wife had become the possessor of an official, but tame, delusion. He has, as the doctors would say, learned to dissociate himself from his wife's symptoms. For her part, the mother has grown coy and vain about her small claim to distinction. When Carl teases her, she brushes him off with what seems like self-conscious pride.

Well, how extremely interesting!

The son-in-law becomes available for long confidential sessions. He and the woman pair off in a corner, exchanging intimate murmurs, and if she suspects when he excuses himself afterwards and shuts himself away that he is retiring to write up notes, she simply does not care. Because these friendly talks have gone so well, she is persuaded to let him arrange for her to have a frank discussion with her local minister. Scratching his bald head, her son-in-law observes, he wouldn't be surprised if all along she had been suffering from a religious, rather than a medical, condition.

But the meeting with her minister is not a success. She remembers and the clergyman remembers that following the mishap at the lake, he had rushed over to pay a condolence call and found himself without any need to condole and his resurrected parishioner barricaded against him. And she is offended by the advice the minister feels called upon to give.

Get out? Stop keeping to herself? Learn to care more? Find some companionable or charitable interests to share with her husband? Spread herself, be active, get involved? But the more she involved herself, the more the rest of them could claim. As it was, she was being swallowed alive, she was being sliced up like a melon, the fruit was consumed and the seeds spat out. Cannibals, they will all end up by having a piece of her. Eventually the world will have devoured her, like a pear, like an apple.

Driving back from the visit, she is filled with a sullen distaste. Now she knows why she has had so little to do with the clergy, all these years. But Carl enthusiastically wraps himself around the spirit of the message. Self-help and inspirational books begin appearing on their bookshelves, to keep company with the house plants, ornamental clocks, and collection of *National Geographics*. One by one arrive puzzles and games for beguiling the leisure hours. The clicking of dice, rattle of dominoes, slap of cards, Carl's "Got you!" and her keen "Oh no, you don't!" rise above the familiar background cadences of television. Some of these contests for possession of imaginary business enterprises, hotel chains, real-estate holdings, complete cities and states, whole countries and dominions, the earth and its envelope of space grow so fierce that the television is even turned off.

From then on, time moves in and out and up and down. There is a good time when, the weather becoming warm again, they hop into the car every afternoon, hunting down roadside stands that offer thirty-year old glass bottles, wagon wheels, and chipped stoneware jugs. They search out dinky little county fairs; they bone up on local historical-society pamphlets and track down what is left of old pioneers' settlements and Indian burial mounds. They make an effort to woo back into their lives a few of their former acquaintances. But some apparently harbor grievances from the time when the housewife shut her door against them; nowadays an awkwardness falls like dust as soon as guests arrive, and neither can Carl's dashing about with glasses in his hands nor the woman's stepping forward to point out the log cabin patchwork quilt or the latest painted tin tray she has picked up at a trash-and-treasures sale, pump life into their gatherings.

To compound the problem, some of the people they once saw, like the old doctor and his wife, have sold out and retired to less bracing climates, others are simply no longer on the scene and, for the present at least, not to be resurrected. The country club is filled nowadays with younger families, it is too crowded and noisy, the children are not well-behaved and the adults run around half-undressed. When they stop to exchange words with an old acquaintance, the hello does not blossom into any more familiar greeting. Wondering why she and Carl are so rarely called, why their invitations are seldom returned, they conclude that people have gotten out of the habit of seeing them. Or, she thinks, recognizing the power that she inadvertently wields, the neighbors have become too wary.

Up and down, round and about.

Another good time when she flies off to both coasts, rebounding from one daughter to the other, carrying a suitcase full of gifts that have been selected after agonies of indecision. These visits are a success, even though the presents have to be brought back for exchange because she has got the children's sizes, ages, and sexes all mixed up.

There follows another whole summer she spends indoors, refusing to leave their air-conditioned house. She is bothered by the heat and glare, the flies and other insects, the odors of the flowers and bushes, the noise of children and dogs playing a half-mile away, the fear that someone may drive up and corner her, unable to escape and at a total loss for conversation.

There is a time still less satisfactory when she starts to pick fights with Carl, accusing him of misplacing or throwing away things she cannot immediately put her hands on. Some of the objects have never to his knowledge been in their possession, and others were left behind with no regret on the occasion of their several moves.

Her inordinate longing for these items freezes up his last reserves of sympathy. The sheer unreasonableness of her need makes him want to strike out at her. Why should she *want* a rusty old eggbeater? A tin washboard? A bag of wooden clothespins? A broken wheelbarrow once used for hauling in kindling?

"What did you do with the hand-operated coffee grinder we used to have? I've looked and can't find it anywhere."

"Did you see me throwing it out?"

"If I didn't," she says evenly, "you must have thrown it away behind my back."

"Oh, for God's sake."

"I know what happens when you get started. You can't stop till you get your way."

"Now, cut that out, will you?"

"Well, would you give me a hand moving the living-room couch?"

"For what reason," he asks, lowering his newspaper.

"I'm looking for a pair of embroidery scissors that must have fallen behind."

"Is it a pair of scissors that you own, or used to own? Or that somebody else used to own?"

"Never mind, I'll remember that you refused to help. By any chance, did you pick them up yourself?"

"Damn, damn!" He slams the paper to the floor and stamps.

The board games are beginning to pall, or the two of them are just not compatible enough to sit for hours pushing tokens around to make up words or recomposing the scrambled pieces of famous and fragmented artworks. In a sense, the quarrels are an improvement over the games, more inventive and bracing. They offer greater promise of excitement and an intimation of shared danger. But when she insinuates

59

that the mailman is holding back letters that should be arriving from their daughters; when she abruptly gives the housekeeper notice after unsuccessfully searching for an old cameo ring that Carl has not seen her put on for twenty-five years; when, after sending the help away, she refuses to let a delivery boy or telephone repairman ride up their driveway, when she waits each morning at the mailbox and denounces the mailman for bringing nothing of interest, when she sends every innocent delivery boy packing, charging toward him like fate with flying hair and awkward curses, when she settles into another hunger strike, and refuses to take in anything more substantial than apple juice and crackers – then Carl is forced to give in to the repeated urgings of his daughters and see to it that this time his wife receives proper medical attention.

9

IT IS SHORTLY after sunset on a radiant evening in June, and the old man and his wife are sitting in half-darkness in the eastern wing of their establishment. If they were to unwind the louvers and open the drapes, they would have transparent sky on the verge of condensing into night. At the opposite end of the house, they would have a ripe afterglow with bands of opal, salmon, maroon shifting across a blue-green ground. Out there the flowering hawthorne shakes the last light off its ruddy branches, a towhee practices trills, a few dogs bark.

Facing away from the outdoors display, the elderly couple are watching a huge wall screen, subdivided into light panels. The birdsong filters through like flaws in the ventilating system. Unfortunately, the live show out there conflicts with a series of programs they are accustomed to watching at this hour, and it would take more than a spectacular sunset, something on the scale of the eruption of Mauna Loa, to change this routine.

Anyway, watching television is one of the few activities, along with eating and exchanging a couple of words during the day, they are still capable of sharing. With both of them grown so deaf, conversation has become self-defeating and is reserved for only the most essential communications and complaints. As a substitute, the several television sets and wall installations are turned on first thing in the morning and left on all day, going through their motions in empty rooms or rooms where people are passing through.

At first glance, the woman appears to have aged less than the man, at least she has kept something bright-eyed, admonitory, almost baleful about her, whereas he has grown more sunken, feeble, and slack, shaky on his feet, apprehensive about his health, yellowed in the face. Everyone remarks how inactive he has become. She is dressed in the style followed by younger women only a season or so ago, but not even the old men, nowadays, go about looking the way Carl does.

It is a small irony in their lives that the man's hearing, far more impeded, is not correctable in any way, whereas his wife's lesser disability might be overcome if she would allow herself the use of a discreet appliance no bigger than a bean. As a result of her stubborn unwillingness to be helped, they have both learned to be fairly adept lip-readers for purposes of television. Tonight, however, he suspects that out of perversity she is wearing her appliance: she is also wearing a pastel woolen shawl over her shoulders, as protection against the rigors of the indoor climate.

The woman gets up and casts a reassuring glance at a monitor box set into the wall, which houses an eternally burning small red bulb like a votive light, a signal that their interconnected alarm system is in operation. Everybody in the community subscribes to this service, which links each home with a central console at police headquarters. More, through Carl's foresight and ingenuity their place has become a maze of the latest, most delicate components and sensing devices: magnetic units installed at the doors and windows, ultrasonic and photoelectric equipment to spy out unwelcome presence inside the rooms, pressure-sensitive mats hidden under carpets to catch the weight of an unwary stranger's feet – in addition to the charged barbed-wire fence enclosing the entire grounds.

It has become a chore to remember to deactivate the devices whenever either of them opens a door or a window or steps into an empty room. Living in hourly fear of setting off false alarms, the old man and woman have come to feel almost like prisoners inside their house, or like cultists whose peculiar rituals and devotions are everlastingly witnessed by that small red light.

Deactivating the alarm, the woman pulls aside the window covering and peers into the deepening night.

"Stop fussing. Nobody's out there."

"Yes, and I bet you could hear if they were!"

Her husband does not turn his head. Closing the heavy drapes, the woman flicks on the powerful outdoor beam that throws a glare many times brighter than daylight over their lawn. This floodlight, inside which their house seems to shrink and huddle in on itself, is kept burning all night. Before returning to the screen she pulls her shawl tighter, and taps a dial on the wall.

Her husband reluctantly turns his face from the newscast. "Stop fussing with the thermostat. It doesn't do any good. I've told you a thousand times."

"I was only making an adjustment."

She fights to be heard above the announcer's voice. It hardly makes a difference: it is a stock response to a stock outburst. Actually, the sound is turned up altogether too loud, it is fortunate that they have no close neighbors.

Not only is there nobody in the vicinity whom loud noises coming from their house might annoy, it is by now absolutely guaranteed that no one will ever come close enough to be disturbed by them, for who would turn up a driveway, past the barriers, to seek out a couple this far advanced in age with a reputation for being inhospitable and a little *too* peculiar?

In one of the lighted panels an announcer with a pointer stands in front of a map and speaks of distant regions and provincial capitals, which formerly neither man nor wife would have heard of, let alone known how to pronounce or spell. By now, grown blasé about the latest battles and campaigns, they peacefully assimilate the most advanced crises and catastrophes, along with the remains of supper in their stomachs. This night, as the woman follows the moving pointer, she becomes aware of a familiar sensation deep inside her, resembling a muffled blast or massive rockslide, followed by a crash and upheaval of powdery debris. Somewhere rubble pelts down a mountain. A good-sized part of her suddenly detaches itself and breaks free, she feels it dropping like a cliff falling headlong into the ocean. It is followed by a frightening sensation of loss.

Two trips to a private hospital and several courses of treatment, however, have taught the patient to keep her private sensations to herself. Besides, more than anything, she is tired. She waits for the terrifying feeling to pass, then acting out a seldom-practiced impulse, she gets up and rests one hand familiarly on the back of Carl's chair. He does not look up.

She sits down again and fusses with a control switch.

"Leave it, will you? Why are you always switching channels?"

"I was only making an adjustment."

This time, with a strong effort she pulls herself together and takes up her work.

Currently the hobbyist is engaged in crotcheting a little woolen star, which will be joined to other stars and stitched into a multicolored bedspread. She has created bedspreads for both daughters, has covered the maidenly beds of three young granddaughters, and has presented gifts of her handiwork to the various nieces and all her sisters-in-law. Her coverlets are raffled off for the benefit of community-chest drives, the flawed ones are shipped to the local thrift shop, the two most splendid and ambitious examples (incorporating the appropriate emblems) have been presented to the State Capitol and the White House, for which she has received thanks on official, embossed stationery.

Their own home has been turned into a bazaar or central repository for colorful, hand-crotcheted throws, covering every lounging facility and flat surface that can accommodate them. Upstairs in the guest-room closets, wrapped in tarpaper against moths, are downy piles of pink and blue baby blankets, whipped up in a matter of hours and put away against some future happy event.

Carl has had to resign himself to finding stray woolen threads clinging like caterpillars to the rugs and furniture and his clothes. He no longer notices the unassembled pieces piled on chairs and tables, waiting to be joined into one lightning-jagged or boldly rectangular or softly undulating pattern.

It is a skill that the woman picked up during one of the expensive hospital stays, which turned out to be almost a form of apprenticeship in the craft, and one she is not likely to abandon. She may have a little trouble at times remembering the names of the recipients, but she will not be diverted from her labors in their behalf.

At the moment, the woman is putting the last touches on a queen-sized blanket that she hopes to have ready for the marriage of her oldest granddaughter, out West. Already she has turned down an invitation to this wedding, although, as her daughter Emmy wrote, it might be their one chance to meet the bridegroom. The way young people moved around these days, who knew when you would catch up?

However, working steadfastly at the gift, the grandmother has as steadfastly refused. Possibly because, in addition to the fatigues of traveling, she dreads having to remember a new name? Or because she hopes that if she fails to make an appearance she may be lucky enough to forfeit a certain souvenir?

Her moving hands set into motion a chain of heart-shaped bangles dangling from her wrist, each heart engraved with a name, a date of birth, and an individual's relationship to herself. A gold heart for the husband; one each for the daughters, the daughters' husbands, and the six lovely grandchildren. Interspersed among the golden, silver hearts for each of the remaining brothers, their wives, her nieces and nephews, her grandnieces and grandnephews, and her one – no, two – great-grandnephews.

This adds up to a considerable number of ornaments to have hanging around one's wrist. Neither she nor Carl is particularly fond of this bracelet, which she fastens on each morning with the enthusiasm of an ox stepping into its yoke, but they dislike it for different reasons.

Carl is annoyed because the bracelet makes a jingling or a clanking noise whenever she moves her hand. It sets up a mindless tinkling with every turn of the crotchet hook; it clanks against pots and utensils as she pokes around in the kitchen; as she sits over her food it taps loudly on her water glass. And because he has no trouble receiving this one sound, although he is blocked off from so much else, Carl doubly resents it and imagines he hears it at times when his wife is sleeping or lying down or definitely not using her arm, or is nowhere in the vicinity.

For her part, his wife dislikes the heavy ornament because it is no joy to wear for someone with delicate bones and arthritic joints, and also because she is uncomfortable at having so many people's names fluttering around her wrist. However, it was sent to her on the occasion of her seventieth birthday as a joint transcontinental offering by both daughters, and at considerable expense, so for three years she has put it on every morning.

He leans over and jabs her knee. "That's taking you forever. Are you going to get it done in time for Teresa's wedding?"

"I think so. I'm almost ready to put it together."

A pause.

"Then you're bringing it with you?"

"What?" Stalling for time, she fingers her appliance. He repeats his question. Twice.

"No" – she finally shouts back – "we'll have to send it along with your check."

He gets up and walks off. "All right, if that's how you want it."

She shouts, to soften the disappointment, "I'm afraid I'm not up to that much traveling."

"If that's how you want it."

Bow-legged, he stumps down to his study.

Now he is gone, the woman fingers her chair arm, hesitating over the multiple channels that will only send back harshly tinted, endlessly repeated variations of herself. She is aware that out there they are constantly stealing away pieces for their own amusement and diversion. When she least expects it, she will find her own face staring out from the screens, her husband, her family, her house, her life story, opinions, shames, secrets carefully smothered and held back until this moment – all exhibited like so many pieces of soiled and savagely ripped bedding. However, two sojourns at a private hospital have convinced her of the wisdom of keeping her insights and intuitions to herself.

She knows the cars hurtling across the plains and deserts carry away her dismembered parts in their trunks, the trailer trucks roaring up the approach ramps spread false rumors by backfire and anguished airbrakes. The satellites and space

platforms keep her in constant dizzying rotation. Planes jut-
ting across the sky incise versions of her history, when they
let go their trails the plumes write out her name in a clumsi-
ly forged hand. But she has learned the hard way not to ven-
tilate her complaints.

Oh, out there they are chattering, chattering, having
nothing better to do, gossiping, spreading the word. Not seeing her, the neighbors make up new, outrageous explanations;
she is reported breaking her back, walking out on Carl after
a fight, flying West when a son-in-law is killed in a crash.

She is rumored to be the last person in the community
seen in conversation with a woman who has mysteriously
disappeared, it is claimed that she is a specialist in palmistry
and black magic.

She is known to carry on a correspondence with people
high in government, to whom she has written letters concerning her neighbors. She is slanderously accused of not being on speaking terms with either of her daughters.

Carl wanders in from the kitchen, carrying a cup of tea
he has made for himself. Looking at him, she feels yet another
segment slip away, rise and take flight like a migrating bird
to some place where it will be shaken down into a new pattern that will be essentially the same. Wrenched hurriedly
away; lured, kidnapped, or stolen.

"I can't get you to change your mind?" he asks without
much conviction.

She pantomimes an answer, shaking her head from side
to side.

Thinking she has not heard, he repeats the question.

Pulling herself together, she shouts, "The package can take
the trip instead of us!"

Looking down at the woman, he does not think, was it
so long ago?

Looking up at the man, she does not think, it passed like
a dream.

"I'm chilly," she says to him. "You always keep it too cold around here. I'm going to get myself some tea too."

She hitches up the cashmere stole brought back by her youngest daughter from Scotland the summer before, and shakes her head. Soon, she thinks, she will belong to the world and everyone in it.

ROYAL BONES

1 Overgrowth

I WAS TOO TALL to be a princess. Too tall and by far too undistinguished. Years of gymnastics and eurythmic dancing never strengthened my backbone to the point where it could support a regal posture. Round-shouldered, long-necked, morbidly shy, I hunted out inconspicuous corners to hide in at receptions and fetes, so far as it was ever possible for me to be inconspicuous. By the age of fifteen, I stood taller than the tallest member of the household guard in his imposing chin-strapped fur shako.

I grew too fast, as a child, for them to keep up with my wardrobe. A week after a dress had been made to measure, the sleeves would be creeping up my arms, the waistline rising inexorably toward the armpit. My appearance, the ridiculous and shabby figure I cut wherever I showed myself, drew comment as a national scandal.

I was considered too delicate for ordinary activities. Fragile as porcelain, at one time or another I must have broken every bone in my body. The first time I sat on a horse, I broke

71

my coccyx; the second time I picked up a badminton rac-
quet and took a swipe at the shuttlecock, I fractured my wrist.
A croquet mallet, inadvertently lowered, smashed my big
toe. I managed to break a leg while stooping to fasten my
iceskates, and my Great-Uncle Hungerford, whom I adored,
drawing me toward him in an affectionate bearhug, cracked
fourteen ribs at one stroke. During my period of most rapid
growth, I walked, sat, limped, or lay swathed in bandages,
a living mummy.

A princess, even seventh in line, should have something
about her notable, rare, distinctive; but I was awkward,
moody, silent, reserved, ungifted, disagreeable, friendless, ill-
regarded, considered stupid (though I was not), unaware of
any potentiality except for growth. And this potentiality I
exercised. And exercised. A prodigy in the one direction, I
excelled only at my prodigiousness. A lonely child, at first
looked on with alarmed amazement, then pitied, then
somehow blamed: as if I had been capable of choice. Crude
teasing, nowhere any understanding, much misery. Accusa-
tions: "When are you going to stop growing?" Wouldn't I
have stopped? By any conceivable act of will?

There wasn't a day when I did not secretly try. On my
ninth birthday, a diary entry in a determined childish hand:
"Nine years old today and as tall as Mama — I'm afraid a bit
more! Otherwise a lovely birthday. The people came with
offerings, etc. The girl who handed me the bouquet giggled.
They say she is old enough to be married, and she only comes
to my shoulder. Gifts from Mama, the court, my cousins,
aunts, sisters, and darling Marina [my nurse]. But not the
gift I want the most. Being promised you know what. Well,
I *am* going to stop. So remember! No nonsense! That door-
post I measure myself against every morning — my head is
not going to reach above the last mark. Ever!"

Well, my head did soon reach above the mark. It was un-
precedented. It was considered inappropriate. It was disastrous.

Even the seventh of a king's eight daughters – Monica, Norma, Sophronia, Althea, Consuela, Thelma, Tall Ille, and baby, Pepita – even one so remote in line should be capable of exercising more control, of showing a better sense of proportion. Of what use then were lineage and tradition, if not to set the example? What in heaven's name was the monarchy for?

And for a while, you know, I did my best to show restraint. Reasoning that if nourishment were cut off, the whole organism might become discouraged, like a plant that is stunted when deprived of sun and water, I tried to limit my intake drastically. But no use. At best, my appetite was voracious, I was capable of putting away at a meal as much as a pair of drovers. If I tried to turn back dishes at the table, an hour later I would be begging food from the kitchen. I would look at village children with hungry eyes, as they ran by with a piece of bread in their hands.

This need for food! Worse than any cottager's child, the craving was never satisfied. Not a moment in my childhood when I was not aching for more. The great platter it took two footmen to carry in and set before dear Mama, who dispensed portions serenely to her brood and all her dependents – did anyone guess how avidly Tall Ille desired for herself the entire juicy browned carcass? If possible, I would have sprung up like a wolf and carried the animal off in my jaws. As it was, I devoured my meals, was constantly admonished to eat more slowly, cadged second and third servings with piteous looks, pretended not to notice the alarmed glances of those who had begun to connect the way I ate with the rate I was shooting up.

But what difference would it have made? If I had eaten any less, I would have starved to death, and the outcome, even for them, so much the more scandalous. Meanwhile, somewhere was a land, somewhere lay a country where my needs and dimensions were a blessing, not a scandal. (This land so far I have never found.) But at ten, as tall as a tall man, and dressed in men's clothing, I saddled a horse and almost reached the frontier before colliding with a farm cart at a crossing. I tumbled off, my long hair coming loose under the cap. The entire mystery surrounding the accident, my lack of identification papers, my childish sobbing, and my shrieks of pain at the border village resulted in a call to the national police who carried me home, feverish, in disgrace – and with a broken collarbone.

Strange, but this is the only attempt at escape I remember, although there must have been others. I suppose there was a peak of misery, which gradually subsided. Slowly, in our different ways, we all made peace with my condition. And what else could anyone have done? Only later were we informed that something might have been done. But at the time, small-minded and complacent, my relations found it easier to gossip about me as an outsize national disaster than to search for a cure. And I, from an early age, laid the responsibility squarely on my mother, who, determined that at this seventh opportunity she was going to deliver a boy but afraid to see the proof of the issue, simply would not let go. She carried me for a full nine months, then a tenth, and might have gone on for the eleventh, except for a holiday fireworks display that went off, all at once, too close to the royal palace. I arrived in a hail of rockets and roman candles, the night sky lit up by rosettes, pinwheels, and giant serpents of fire, writhing and exploding together. . . . A national disaster, which, except for biological incident or God's will might have been the longed-for benefit, and an occasion for wildest rejoicing.

None of my sisters made her entry to the tune of royal fireworks. All of them were born prematurely – Monica, Norma, Sophronia, Althea, Consuela, Thelma, and then, after me, Pepita. Carried for a few short months and then ejected from the cockpit, tossed casually into life to lie swathed in blankets and hastily devised incubators until like little red eggs they were ready for hatching. Each one outgrew the bad timing and arrived at young womanhood with the right collection and arrangement of properties: a series of round, blooming, delicate, well-proportioned, appealing, dimpled, giggling, squealing, gravely dignified, fair-browed princesses of the blood. They were so similar, so close to striking the same note, that people had difficulty telling them apart. While they were growing up, they had seemed like different stages in the life of one person. Visitors coming back to court after an absence of years were always confusing one with another, to be answered with a delicious giggle: "I'm not Norma, Cousin, I'm Consuela!" or, "Don't you recognize me, Uncle, I'm Sophronia. I sat on your lap when I was five years old and played with your chiming watch!" In family photographs of parties, picnics, outings; grouped stolidly on yachts or waving from small skiffs or playing lawn games, dressed in the flouncing muslins of the period or nautical in broad straw hats and striped jerseys — well, here they are, an assortment of select, well-graded beauties. And one upstanding stalk among all those nubile berries.

Eight daughters to be married off — and only so many suitable candidates in all Europe. Eight daughters to be married, and never enough money in the national treasury: all those weddings, those dowries, the state festivities, Papa's runs of bad luck at Monte Carlo, Mama's health crises, the frequent confinements, and the succession of cures at smart spas, where a style of life had to be kept up that would not throw discredit on the nation. The unbroken horse he mounted after drinking a liter of aquavit that did Papa in and ended the threat of an unending supply of little princesses. . . . A medium-sized kingdom, the people naturally wanting and expecting more for themselves every year, and each year seeing no gain in produce except in princesses: why should anyone care about one royal marriage more or less?

One after the other, the girls, even Pepita, were married off, amidst appropriate festivity, if with diminishing expense. I grew used to each new brother-in-law's startled looks, his reassuring glance over to his own Consuela, his Sophronia. All of them married, and I still gazing warily out of the nest. Seven perfectly-formed buds, and one spiky branch; seven plump quails, and one gaunt ibis. No, as I'll tell you, seven nesting hens and one flamingo.

At court, I think they were relieved when I refused, with a braying laugh I have since learned to repress, the few matches they had been able to propose. These few suitors, bribed, intimidated, or otherwise induced, were without exception so feeble, insipid, or loathsome, that they would have been an imposition not only on me but on the social resources of the court. There was also the fear that the condition might be hereditary. Someone remembered a great-great-aunt on my father's side who had been nearly my size but who had hardly ever been seen, because of the intolerant and prudish attitudes of her time. A virtual recluse, she furnished a suite of rooms with oversize furniture and refused to step out of them or allow anyone in, except for leaving trays in the serving pantry. With the shutters permanently closed and the only light coming down through a clerestory window, she convinced herself at last that she inhabited the only world there is, and died quite mad, in a welter of dust, rags, decaying food scraps. Whereas I — I have been about, have had interesting adventures away from home, and have constructed a useful life.

Here in my own country, I'm afraid that the people never took to me. The people were ashamed of me. The people made fun of me. They were rather unkind. Of the epithets that followed me on the street, on my way to and from the Institute for Daughters of the Aristrocracy, the most generous was "Stork." Giraffes, of course, I have always admired, and on subsequent visits to Africa I have often watched through binoculars the passage of these graceful creatures across the flat band of the earth, waving their long necks that allow them to reach the most succulent leaves on the trees. . . . But at home the general population was aligned against me, and they were as happy as I when, my education finished, I decided to leave.

By then, my health had greatly improved. Much, much too late, specialists had been called in and glandular treatments begun. My growth slowed down and finally stopped. In one year I grew less than an inch, then the next year not quite that, then between my eighteenth and nineteenth birthdays – rejoice! – not at all. The long ordeal was over. As my bones hardened, my stamina picked up, and eventually I was able to take on as much as the next woman: perhaps more. But by that time, of course, it was too late to do anything about my height but accept it.

On the specialists' advice, I was encouraged to accommodate myself to my condition and whatever limitations it might impose, to move about as I liked, to enjoy myself in a subdued fashion suited to my responsibilities, appearance, and situation in life. I grew up into a faintly ridiculous young lady, catastrophically tall, full of reverent opinions and quaint enthusiasms, dashing forward one minute, retreating the next, eager, abashed, savagely opinionated, melting and tremulous over high-minded expressions of belief. No one thought of standing in the way of my respectable ardor for the sciences, my pursuit of ethnology and archeology.

Ashamed that more had not been done for me while there had been a chance, the court allowed me full travel expenses, with the understanding that no one would interfere with my researches and that I might travel about alone. After all, they asked, who was going to accost *me* on a dark night?

And I am happy to report that no one ever has.

2 Full Measure

HERE YOU HAVE a studio photograph, taken just before I pulled myself together and escaped. See how I am shrinking back on the velvet ottoman, dressed in old-maidish clothing a full decade behind the current fashion, in disagreeable dull colors that are supposed to make the wearer less conspicuous, whereas all they accomplish is to add a vague discomfort to whatever else she may be feeling. But even then, stiff, soulful, dreadfully shy, corseted, parasoled, white-kid-gloved, with one hand resting on a plaster bust of Dante – even at the time I was supported by the knowledge that underneath those unimpressive garments was a sight to evoke in the beholder a certain wonderment, possibly a kind of awe. And in the years to follow, there were enough who did stop and pay their tribute, when I was still vain enough to care about collecting this type of offering.

If you know anything of those years, then you have heard of Princess Ille, Madcap Ille, often in disguise but undisguisable. After my delayed entry into the world, I took a deep breath and became another person. Not all at once; but little by little a different Ille emerged, muffled and covered up by her previous existence as the naked Ille had been camouflaged by her outlandish clothes, and as her exceptional bones had been swathed like a bride in yards and yards of impeccable pale satin.

Being able to get away and travel was very good for me. It gave me the relative point of view that is so essential. My interests took me to many countries, and after I learned to expect being gawked at wherever I went, being the tallest person in any crowd, being tapped on the shoulder at the theatre and politely asked to sit down in my seat . . . I made the necessary adjustments and tried to fit myself to the limits of the other passengers on the ark. Wherever possible I took a box to myself at the theatre, or sat in the last row. I learned to perch contorted and folded up like an umbrella, in places of public accommodation. As for hotel beds, there was the amusing expedient of adding a chair or two to the foot. But wagons-lits were a punishment, and I was glad when air travel finally arrived. I was one of its earliest enthusiasts and for a while kept and flew my own light plane.

Still, I must admit, it took years before I felt easy about being incessantly stared at. I had to learn to absorb the shock in people's eyes when they first caught sight of my feet, the length of my fingers. The Mediterranean ·countries were always the worst. My appearance on a street was enough to produce volleys of cheers and whistles from the men, while heads popped out of windows and little children came running up to lay on a hand —

At the beginning, this kind of thing, when severe, led to a hasty flight back to my rooms, and departure from town by the next train. But finally, realizing that no matter how I tried to hide, people were going to stare anyway, that concealment in my case was impossible unless I became invisible, I decided to give them something worth staring at. Far from being restricted, you see, I had been given a freedom beyond other women. I threw away my governessy wardrobe and put on anything that appealed to me, suitable or not for the occasion. I did not flinch at tossing a Tyrolean jacket over a tremendous ruffled gypsy skirt when attired in my most severely expensive *costume tailleur;* or adding boots and an ostrich-plume cape to a Highlander's Black Watch kilt. I composed unheard-of color combinations. I let my hair hang down and dyed it, sometimes several shades at once. I stalked, I fancy, like a great bird through galleries and historic sites, pleased at last when I captured the attention that had been claimed for centuries by the Blue Mosque in Istanbul or by Michelangelo's *David.*

Away from the dowdy atmosphere of our court, the dreary dinners at the long table with my mother and my seven sisters, until one by one (even little Pepita), they were married off; away from my aunts, cousins, second cousins, deadly respectable ladies-in-waiting – all this behind me, I learned that food was more than a pallid remedy for hunger, that dancing was more than high-minded curative exercises. So many good things to eat, drink, see, hear, touch, do! Fragrant dishes that I might immerse myself in, sit down to eat and eat. A magnum of champagne to be drunk at a meal to the accompaniment of my companions' clapping and good-hearted *bravas*. Dances that were spirited, fast, audacious, consuming, trancelike, abandoned, elegiac. Myself, shawled in tiers from neck to ankles, dancing alone one night in the center of a floor to the ghostly castanet click of the cicadas.

And talents previously unsuspected: my flair for languages, my ability to orient myself at once, so that I feel at home anywhere in the world. A reputation as a great-hearted buffoon and fantastic improvisor, a tireless originator of games and entertainments, a reliable judge of fine dishes and wines. So many extraordinary people to be known: to go off with on amusing expeditions, to sail with, one midnight off Antibes, on a drunken picnic in an approaching gale, from which only by the grace of the drunk or the damned do we return alive. And talented friends to join with, in our more serious moments, in supporting – did I mention that I was an ardent patron of the Russian ballet? Here I am, posed between Diaghilev and the doomed Nijinsky, like a huntress standing between two small-scale exotic specimens. In those seasons when brilliance rolled like a burning carriage over the map of Europe, I rolled with it – like the others imagining that I was a free-moving member of the procession, although who knows, we may all have been prisoners, shackled to its passage.

I have been married many times; unofficially, of course. In different places, to different partners. It makes me a little uncomfortable now to admit that at first I deliberately flushed out my suitors. Noticing in the papers that an athlete of exceptional stature had arrived in town, hearing of an outsize wrestler or prodigious strong man, I would send off an obliquely worded note on crested paper, inviting the champion to call at my hotel, where, out of curiosity or in the hope of raising a little cash, he would invariably turn up. And so I became acquainted with skilled combatants and Olympic medal holders, men of remarkable aptitude and endurance, who had set records for throwing, tossing, hurling, jumping, forcing their fellows to the mat, or speeding like death-bent icebirds down dangerous slopes of snow. I learned that even here, among this special element of the population, one could not safely set rules: some of the men who turned up before me, red-faced and grinning, were the clumsy low-minded opportunists one might have expected, but others were dignified and calm, gentle in spite of their great strength, slow-moving, with classical profiles; wise when uneducated (and some highly educated), proud of their accomplishments but by no means claiming all the credit, deferring admirably to the contributions of teamwork and group spirit. . . . Not one of them could measure up to me in height. Oh, I admit it does seem literal minded and arbitrary, setting up an insensitive yardstick in matters where delicacy and the widest play of inclination should prevail but, before passing judgment, ask yourself what you would have done in my situation.

I may as well confess that before learning to take these things as they came, I kept expanding my searches, always in the one narrow direction. I hunted down prodigies and statistical marvels. I presented myself to side-show performers and traveling exhibitionists – faulted, gaunt, ugly men, not smoothly put-together the way I was – and as often as not was rebuffed, because the strongest affinity of their hearts was for someone moderate and commonplace, a girl on the model of my own sisters.

In the course of years of considerable moving about, I made many acquaintances among celebrities and a horde of commonplace people. The Glamorgan Giant for a time was a special friend of mine, though I was put off by his accent and professional country-bumpkin style. For one season I was stricken by the tallest member of the Buckingham Palace guard. Day after day I stood watching him, the two of us sweltering in an exceptionally torrid London summer. It would hardly have done for me to make the overtures (related as we were to the Royal Family), and *he* never once lowered his eyes from the blazing sky to level them some few inches above his own.

Eventually I became such an expert on the relative highs and lows of the world's population that I could recite like a prayer where the heaviest concentration of tall people might be found from country to country, and within each country's borders. Reasoning that it was time I marry and settle down, I yearned for a place of my own – an island would have done – where there was a certain number of men whom I might look in the eye. Where I might find a choice and, within this choice, anonymity. So crossing mountains, rivers, oceans, continents, rushing from one time zone to the next, zigzagging the equator . . .

One delightful African sojourn was spent on the Rwanda highlands among the elongated, patrician Watusi. Because I was white, foreign, dressed in khaki bush clothes and pith helmet, and carrying a camera and an old-fashioned machine for recording ceremonies it became an accepted myth that I was not really a woman. So I was allowed to join the men, grazing the longhorn cattle, singing, dancing, spending hours in the shade drinking the local beer, while the women toiled in the sun. At night I was passed down the line, being given, giving myself, to whomever they – or I – might please. And I have this to say for myself, both here and elsewhere, that what I was given, I gave back; and whatever was offered me, I returned, full measure. Recurrent sunstroke and an inability to digest fermented milk finally convinced me that it was time to leave. Regretfully I stalked away, camera on my back and my hunting rifle slung over my shoulder, accompanied by friendly salutes from my distinguished, supple, tall, black next-of-kin.

Too difficult – to list the extent of the wandering I passed through before giving up all hopes of finding a hero and a province of my own. Before settling for the world as it is, I flung myself despairingly at the limits. I tried to stretch the boundaries of space and time. Running down stories of legendary Tall Men who had in the remote past inhabited the region, I arrived one summer in the green Dordogne valley, where descendants of the original full-statured, long-headed Cro-Magnon were said now and then to crop up among the local farmers. I never managed to locate even one of these recidivists, but to this outing I owe the throwing overboard of amateurism and the launching, some years later, of my professional career: serious field trips, years of study at distinguished universities, a scholarly enthusiasm for tracking down the unrecorded movements of the early peoples, and my specific aptitude for recognizing and cataloguing those bits of weaponry and bone that are sometimes the only traces by which you can follow the great flux and flow over the continents. My ecstatic exploration continued to flower, long past the heavy green summer when I first haunted the caves where the ancient hunters painted the chase and laid down their bones.

But before the effervescent Ille could transform herself into the specialist and meticulous researcher as she is known in the world today, there were a few minor paths yet to be followed, branching off the well-worn road. One gets so tired of sameness! One begins to hope that the opposite can bring release. And an obsession too quickly repudiated, you know, is always in danger of toppling over into the other corner: which is how it happened with me.

You may remember the fable that tells how Zeus, having just finished the job of creating mankind, instructs Hermes to put intelligence into the bodies; how Hermes takes a measure and pours an equal amount of brains into each inert body, so that the small man comes out with more than his fair share, while the bigger fellow is proportionately short-changed. I began to suspect some truth to the tale. Anyway, I was tired of the tall man's Olympian detachment, his ability to see all sides of a question, his instinct for fair play combined with his conviction of innate superiority. I began to have a longing for the small man's devices: cunning, adroitness, resourceful wit. So going straight at it, as I had trained myself, I made a trip to the mountain village in Sicily where some of the shortest people in all of Europe are to be found. During the past hundred years, records demonstrate, not one man from the province has exceeded five feet, and most are considerably smaller.

Arriving in town, I immediately rented a room overlooking the white sun-baked piazza, and let it be known that for the first two weeks a special introductory fee would be charged. They arrived and kept arriving – I was surprised to discover such density of population. For a week, the café under my room was jammed day and night with brawling, diminutive men. The café owner was forced to hire assistant waiters and was going mad with visions of expanding profits. He offered to buy an interest in my person and implied that with his connections, both legal and infra-legal, I had no choice about accepting. It seemed that unless I was willing to launch an international incident, I might never be allowed to leave. I was growing bored and had developed a painful back condition from stooping so far over to converse with my clientele.

Fortunately, the women turned on me one day in a crowd armed with stones and kitchen knives, cursing me up and down as a *strega* and sending me fleeing down the road to Agrigento. Before leaving, I slipped the last of my earnings as a good-will offering to the local padre, who had become my close friend; partly because he was the smallest man I had ever seen; partly because he could beautifully recite long sections from Leopardi; and partly because he had more leisure for conversation than even the men who hung about the cafés.

Immediately afterward, to counteract the taste of this episode, I gave in to long-standing temptation and made a try at a theatrical career. For one season I stood in the chorus line at the Folies Bergères, equipped only with a helmet and a spear. The theatrical agent who discovered me, and got me drunk later that evening on bad champagne was amazed, then outraged, then amused, to discover who I was. He tried his hardest, and eventually I appeared under my own name with a provincial company, performing the tragedies of Racine to packed houses.

After that, because engagements were scarce, I teamed up with a specialized circus that offered diversion in the salons and private clubs of the wealthy. I was partnered with an insane Chinese midget, who took an instant dislike to me and flailed me with his tiny fists when he thought no one was watching. Because I felt persecuted by his murderous threats and was afraid he might really poison me, I pulled out without giving notice, and was startled a few weeks later on one of my rare visits home to realize that a guest who had seemed vaguely familiar at the last performance was my second cousin Albert on my father's side. He seemed bemused by the coincidence too, though naturally neither of us mentioned the city where the exhibition had taken place.

But these deviations lost their novelty. Ways of filling in gaps in the days became harder to come by – the gaps remained. Everything changed. The parties stopped, the brightest people died off, the times became more serious. Just before the war broke out, I gave in to the repeated invitations of an American medical team and flew over to join the staff of a well-known research institute. For two years I lived in a private apartment at the institute, collaborating in all their tests, becoming an intimate friend of several doctors. I learned a great deal about my condition, which strains and stresses my health can support, which to avoid, and what to expect as time went on. Because of my theatrical experience I had no self-consciousness about being exhibited across the country at meetings and conventions, and I keep at my bedside, as a memento of those years, a standard medical text in which I am shown standing naked – in peak condition, though I had just reach my fifty-second birthday – photographed against a black curtain, my eyes blanked out, and a flattering caption printed underneath.

During my American stay, which because of the war dragged out longer than I had planned, I was continually brought up against the pathetic awe that these professed republicans showed for a representative of outworn royalty, though most of the people I met could hardly have told you what continent my country stood on. Working hard to become a part of the life around me, I volunteered for some seasons to perform as a clown at children's hospitals and benefit shows; but I was not a success. Without intending to, I frightened young children – even my nieces and nephews back home were extremely wary of me. Little children were jolted by their first sight of me and rarely unbent later. Perhaps the difference in proportion was really too great for such small beings. Or perhaps something else was at work, some other difference, darkly surmised by children and simple creatures like the peasants back home.

Now that I am growing older, I indulge myself with this kind of thinking.

But really, I am well satisfied with the interests and the life I have built up. Every day I receive in the mail letters from distinguished universities, addressing me as Dear Colleague — by my request, no longer Princess — inviting me to speak at conferences or contribute papers to symposia. When I travel, I consult with museum curators about especially puzzling remains and artifacts. My insights and hunches are sometimes regarded as uncanny. But I cannot help thinking that more than coincidence must have led me toward this field of concentration. See here, my own country had been run-over and overrun so many times in its history that invasion was less than an incident. Rapine and destruction leveled its cities nearly as fast as they were built up. Some pillager or warrior, passing through from the East in his hasty peregrinations, must have been responsible for the odd strain. . . . Who he was, of course, where my kind comes from, will never advance from a mystery to a conjecture.

As for the present, even minor royalty is no longer in fashion. Of my seven sisters, four are dead, and three living abroad in bourgeois propriety. I visit them every year and am saddened to see how they have knuckled under — how they are determined to squeeze out the last drops of comfort. My native land was converted years ago to a system of state socialism, and a fabulous past, I have learned, can carry you just so far. I am grateful that the state budget still finds the funds to keep up my small pension. I suspect the current government is rather fond of me: I appeal to the new guardians as a relic, an anomaly spawned by an anachronistic system, who can always be pointed out as a horrid example when denouncing its flaws. . . . What would they do without me?

When I do go back for an occasional visit I am politely left alone, no notice is taken of my comings and goings — I

87

am not even followed – and a few days before leaving, I am usually visited by a well-mannered, alarmingly well-educated young woman of the proletarian class, who asks politely about my recent travels, inquires if there are any new finds I care to donate to the state museum, and lists the additions to my bibliography. Have I mentioned that within my limited field, my scholarship is quite respected?

For the rest, since I can't think what else to do, I suspect that as long as my strength holds, I will continue pushing these old bones over the earth. There is a situation I intend to look into in Central Anatolia next summer after I finish work on my new book, if I feel I can undertake the journey in that heat. The way things have worked themselves out – really, I can't complain. Starting out as it did, it might have been calamitous, but I've had plenty of good times. Take it all the way it is. There have been worse lives, lesser inventions.

3 Contraction

IT'S A COMMONPLACE observation and a paradox that we all tend to grow a bit shorter, the longer we stay on this planet. The pull exerted on all objects by the earth's core and our human stubbornness in prancing around upright, instead of going it sensibly on all fours, have their cumulative effect. Even the most inflexible military carriage is known to slacken toward the end. With me, the process was sudden, very dramatic. The doctors had forewarned me to expect changes, but nothing they said could have prepared me for the degree of change.

My dressmakers and fitters at the special houses where I have my clothes run up began to advance a few hints as they set down their tape measures and knelt before me, mouths full of pins. Then one day, putting on some old thing I had not worn for years, I was astonished to see how the garment hung down, sagged, and trailed. It was entirely too long all over and might have been cut to fit another person.

There it was: the special character of my bones and my habitually poor posture had speeded up a process common to everyone. Between my sixtieth and seventieth birthdays I contracted noticeably; and this, just at a time when the peoples of the world, as a result of better nutrition and improved living circumstances, were tending in the other direction. Just the other day I learned from the newspapers of two individuals, brother and sister, within forty miles of where I live, who definitely outmeasure me. I have lost my claim to distinction and am ending up merely a remarkably tall old lady, of whom I like to think people say, "She must have been handsome in her day. . . ."

In various other ways one begins to notice a cutting-down. That's not exceptional, is it? Though at one time we had hoped it might go on exactly the way it was forever. But would that be so desirable? In the long run? All that wonderful food consumed, bottles emptied, laughter, excursions, introductions, intrigues, secret meetings, hopes violently raised, then muted; then forgotten. All those miles covered – cities, provinces, lights, pictures, magic views. Broken glass, cities smashed to rubble, rebuilt; and all the time processes of digestion going on, slow transformations, excretion, decay. All that mileage covered, that as the earth turns may add up to no more than standing still. . . . And so few of the people who matter left. Let it go.

You may want not to say never, yet you learn to withhold. You don't wish to cut down, but you want to conserve what's left for what may be the most important yet. I notice as time goes on how my tastes have turned more strictly classical; what is not part of the main gesture can be dispensed with. On my travels, I no longer respond to the occasional furtive overtures from camel drivers and muleteers in isolated mountain passes, apart from the other members of the expedition. There's been a diminishment not only in energy, but in ardor. Still to keep making the attempt! These last few years, with all the difficulties, I see where I have been covering more territory than ever. It comes down to a fascinating, brutal, personal, oddly formal contest. You know where you are wanted: and you know what you are after. The truth is there's something rather special I've been lately on the trail of. I may get there while my strength lasts, I may not.

Above the Taurus ranges, an eagle scanned the arid highlands and treeless steppes, the glaring salt flats and mystical patches of green, the grazing lands and distant wheat fields that dipped level by level toward the last mountains and the sea. The sun was going down fast, with a stroke canceling the assault of the day's heat, before the greater assault of the night's cold. I buttoned up my extra sweater and felt in the pocket for my cotton gloves. I unstrapped my canteen and set it down inside the entrance, where I could find it when needed. Then looking again down the steep, almost vertical trail – still no sign of the returning guides or any human presence in this remote pass – I picked up my flashlight, and went back in.

All afternoon I had spent on my hands and knees inside this chamber, measuring, pacing off, taking photos, making detailed drawings and notes. Nothing was left for me to accomplish here. What followed would be for the teams and their specialized equipment. Though less than I'd hope for, the find was important and would fill in gaps; giving comfort to certain of my colleagues, demolishing others. But I had no desire to spend the night at this altitude, in this cold. By now I was more than ready for the men to return.

Already it was hours past the time they had promised I would see them. It had been foolish giving them anything in advance, but at the end they became so wheedling and abusive I handed over part of the dispute fee, just so I could get on with the work. After getting the money out of me they left, promising to come back in the time it took to smoke three cigarettes. Refusing to believe I understood the local dialect, they held up the three middle fingers of their hands; a pair of stubborn, squat, crafty, filthy, petty adventurers, peasants or shepherds got up to look like desperados in their neckerchiefs wrapped halfway up their unshaved jaws and their caps with visors pointing backward. As accommodating and full of good will as the mules we had used on the later stages of the trip. They had taken the mules too – unhitched and led them down the trail, pausing at the first bend to turn around and hold up three fingers for three cigarettes. . . .

Well, allowing for the local time sense, they could have gone through a couple of packs by now. I returned to the mouth of the burial chamber and scanned the rapidly dimming valleys below: no sound, no rising dust, no other hint of movement on the path, not a thing to announce a person or animal making the formidable climb. The chill coming up through the stone porch and the tiredness that follows the exhilaration of discovery simply reaffirmed that it had been a violently difficult day.

Called at four by the first set of drivers, I stumbled through the darkness into the waiting Jeep for the trip to the halfway spot, where we were to make connection with the muleteers. In the course of a two hours' pitch and toss over unpaved roads, we broke down twice, the first time on the edge of a blazing salt flat, the second in a gulley where we choked on ochre dust. Each time my rage seemed disproportionate to the degree of inconvenience. My punished bones and the tremors and giddiness from the ride reminded me that I would not see eighty again.

At their first glimpse of me, the muleteers, squatting on the ground beside their sleepy animals, snickered, and they laughed outright when they saw me climb onto my stubby-

legged carrier and settle in, sidesaddle. On the rougher sections of the path, where the animals stumbled over loose
stones and shale, we were forced to dismount and proceed
on foot. By the time we arrived, the sun was directly over-
head, and I was wilting under my sunglasses and wide-
brimmed hat. I rationed my water supply in anticipation of
a thirsty day, but I had hardly counted on the night.

Yes, even for an experienced traveler it had been a difficult,
exasperating journey. Outraged with the mule drivers because
they demanded three times the amount previously agreed on,
I received a disturbing picture of how I had changed. At one
time, I would have cheerfully offered up anything for the
sake of an hour's entertainment, and here I was nearly letting a small-minded fear of being cheated deprive me of the
bigger thing I was after.

As we plodded on, glimpsing a few far-off villages, clusters
of houses crumbling back into their essential mud; viewing
through the heat haze an occasional farmer far below following his animal and solid-wooden-wheeled cart; winding past
sheer drop-offs, embracing the sides of naked pinnacles –
willingly I conceded that I was too old for this strenuous
foray. What was a woman of my age doing, nodding on the
back of a reluctant animal, in hundred-twenty-degree heat?
No wonder they considered me ridiculous: I was ridiculous.
And after this partial failure and disappointment I was going to give in, and accept the outing as final.

I walked back inside the chamber to make certain I had
not left any gear behind. My camera holder was packed and
strapped, and the burned-out flash bulbs were stowed inside
the pockets. No reason to add contemporary debris to an
ancient depository, though probably more had been removed
from this depository than remained.

Especially during the last stages of the climb, the guides
had been abusive to the animals and unresponsive, secretive,
and insolent with me. Once or twice I suspected they were

trying to maneuver my mule too close to the edge. After that, I made an effort not to doze in my seat. They would beat their mounts, race ahead, and smile insultingly as I caught up, holding on for dear life. Apparently, some business was going on between them that by this late hour I could easily guess. At any rate, until I'd had a chance to publish my reports, their secret was safe with me. Let them come back and finish the job, and I would say nothing about it when I arrived at the capital. At most, I might report that the guides supplied that day had been unpleasant, discourteous, and malicious, to keep an old lady waiting, chilled to the bone and growing apprehensive. . . .

It was still light where I stood, though the valley was in shadow. Light enough to make out, on the rock shelf some hundred feet off the path, the inconspicuous mound of heaped-up stones, the rubble of the mountainside, with a solid stone slab for roof and door. Cut into the face of the mountain and blending with it – you might pass by a thousand times before noticing. Recognizing the heap as man-made, you might take it for an improvised shelter for wandering agricultural laborers. Never for such a permanent and persistent dwelling.

The big mistake was in providing a map of where I wished to be conducted. The possible location of one of these mounds had been nibbling at my mind for years. Poking around the countryside, making inquiries, accepting the hospitality of the people, I had been able to sketch out a likely location with an accuracy that made me proud, but then it had been foolish not to suspect the others would try to get here first.

After grudgingly prying back the entrance slab, the guides had refused to take a step inside, claiming a superstitious terror of what such a sanctuary might contain. They spat, swore, made the sign of the cross and the sign against the evil eye. They implied I would be out of my mind to go in. They tried to delay me by demonstrating in sign language what had happened to individuals who had disturbed similar precincts. Then they delayed me further by unreasonably insisting on an installment on their pay. By the time I was able to pick up my torch and enter, they were gone, with that insulting final gesture of their fingers.

I stooped over to massage my knees and ankles. All my joints were aching after hours of kneeling on hard stone. While there was still much to do, I had not felt how the day had drained my resoures, now I was beginning to realize what the trip had taken out of me. My shuddering was from cold as well as fatigue. The extra sweater offered only a memory of warmth. Really, the men must return very soon, the temperature could go down to the bitterness of a winter night at these altitudes, and I had brought no sleeping bag or blankets or extra food, just those few remaining mouthfuls of water.

Somewhere close by, a bird or night creature ejected one short scream. Farther down, on more benevolent altitudes, wolf caroling, a duet or trio, broke out.

To get some protection from the wind I went back into the burial room. It struck me this time that the air inside was less musty, a bad sign. The door ought to be sealed up immediately, before irreparable damage set in. It may have been twenty-four hours before my own arrival that the slab had first been pulled open, letting in the air of a new day. This sudden change of atmosphere, after so long a time, could make moving about hazardous. An imprudent pressure or an incautious touch could set off a reaction that might shatter the contents and reduce them to powder.

The girls lay where I'd left them, one to either side of the opening into the inner room. Surrounded by a few bronze amulets and bangles, fragments of pottery for serving up and storing food, scraps of fabric, pieces of a bronze mirror, a razor – on call for such duties as slaves or handmaidens might perform in this life or another. The broken bits scattered around the room suggested how rich a trove they must have

94

guarded. Whoever had got up here before me had callous-
ly disarranged and trampled their bones in haste to remove what could be carried off. Disheveled, they lay on
their sides with knees drawn up, their bones still showing traces of a red dye. One girl not eighteen, the other
no more than thirty. Pitiful, if you could read the signs:
their necks had been broken shortly before they were laid
down.

In the inner room the man lay with his head pointing
toward the East. Under the the remarkably well-preserved
black fur robe, the remains were deeply permeated with red
ochre. Most striking about all three was their unusual size.
I had spent all afternoon measuring the long bones, the verte-
brae, the extraordinary hands and feet, making every allow-
ance to be on the conservative side, but there could be no
question. Alive, the two women would have stood shoulder
to shoulder with me at my full height, and the man would
have carried himself a good head higher.

Whoever he may have been, the man in the fur, he had
commanded this sumptuous animal skin robe and the bronze
ax head, signal of authority, placed inside it. The remains
of a finely woven carpet were laid down under what of
necessity must have been a royal bier. For the rest, it was
missing: the kingly diadem, the bow decorated with animal
figures in precious metals, the gold and silver vessels for drinking the enemy's blood, the massive plates incised with stags
and leopards and wild steppe horses.

Although they had not stripped his bones of his last garment, my traveling companions had made off with whatever
of value that could be pirated or peddled, anything that could
identify the inhabitants of this chamber. Too much had been
removed: we would not know much more about them. The
robbers had buried the dead, twice over.

Looking at the man in the fur robe, I drew in my breath
once more and got down on my knees. What difference did

it make that the accouterments were missing? He owned as much as the dead can expect to.

I remained kneeling beside him, the flashlight steady in my hand. I knew who was here and what was between us. I had zigzagged over this small planet. I had traveled by air, ship, train, motorcycle, rickshaw, dogsled, droshky. I had ridden the backs of donkeys, horses, elephants, water buffaloes. I had covered millions of miles to get here, so why should a few millennia between us matter?

But the journey had tired me, more than I'd expected. The men were very late; the chances were that they would not get back tonight. *If I am lucky, I think, they will not find me alive when they return.*

I raise the flashlight above my head, and hurl it as far as I can. I hear metal crash on the stone floor, glass break, the bulb explode. Back in a darkness that has lasted thousands of years, which reaches down to fit me like a garment, I step out of my clothes. Guided by touch, I grope along the floor, peel away the robe and join in a last embrace my own dear naked inapprehensible love.

TROUBLES OF A
TATTOOED KING

1 Self-Exposure

THE FIRST PROBLEM with being a tattooed king is that the people are always expecting us to strip off our royal robes and exhibit more of ourselves than is appropriate to a person in our position. And at any time and at any place. Now, I was brought up to believe that even the round swell of a man's upper arm is a sight that should be reserved for the beach, barracks, playing field, gymnasium, boudoir. And because a man's muscled bicep is a monument to the art of dermal decoration, tastefully worked over by the needles of master technicians, imported from as far away as Yokohama and Rangoon – is no excuse, so far as I'm concerned, for a major lapse in manners.

"Svendlof," my mother used to say to me, "little bearcub, it may turn out that you are the last of our line to have the honor. As you know, we are only a constitutional monarchy. The public's taste is always unpredictable, its whims arrogant and malicious. What the people have given, the people can take away. Some day you may find yourself driving a taxi or, if things go all the way, a tractor. But remember, good manners can never be requisitioned by the state."

Thank the stars my poor mother did not live to see our last celebration of Great Kettle Day. Stripped to my linen shirt with both sleeves rolled as high as the shoulder, standing on a wooden platform in the middle of our public gardens, the military band straining away at our national anthem — overruled by the huge crowd pounding and clanging on thousands of copper kettles — lights, diplomatic representations from every continent, exchanges of courtesies, speeches, flowers, the blank-faced cameras pushed close to the platform, carrying to the screens of people at home and the world beyond the isthmus the image of Svendlof the Vulgar, last of his line, rippling his arms like an acrobat, making each ornamented muscle jump. Then the high point of the performance: the energetic routine of St. George lancing the dragon, tattooed on the right bicep, the routine the people have come to expect and demand.

And all the while I stand there, blinded by lights, deafened by the noise of the crowd tapping their copper kettles with knives and spoons to frighten away the last vestiges of winter; breathing as though I had been running through the mossy countryside for miles, calculating like any trained performer, animal or human, how many seconds more it will take to satisfy them, whether I can get away this time without doing the struggle of Mars and Venus caught in Vulcan's net, tattooed around the right nipple, which unfortunately will mean taking off my shirt.

From the massed throats of the people a catchy buzz swells to a murmur. A roar grows in strength until the crowd becomes one single, gaping mouth: "Svendlof! Son of Olaf! Grandson of Petrof! Descendant of Borof! Descendant of Svirdlof! Descendant of Olaf the First! Petrof the First! Last Descendant of the First Borof! Svendlof!"

Now I know it is over. I can smile, extend a much-decorated

royal hand, tattooed inside and out, above their heads, roll down my sleeves, smile once more, and step off the platform. Thanks to my acquired gifts and my accumulated self-sacrifices, the royal house has been preserved for another year. The band starts playing, the people slowly fan off toward their houses. I too can leave. Escaping the horde of international visitors, leaving their reception and entertainment to my ministers, I wander off from the public gardens, an inconspicuous figure in my hooded waterproof. It begins to rain, mildly at first, then pelting, the downpour that usually breaks up Great Kettle Day. The bunting droops from the platform, the royal colors bleeding and washing away. Even if I were to bare myself to the skin in a public place—a ceremony I am forced to endure once every five years—if I were to run naked through this rainstorm of nearly tropical invective, none of those acquisitions that mark me off from other men would be washed away. Resigned to my differences, then, taking a wan pride in them, I move off from the grounds. If there were only more gratitude in this world! The water sloshes down the hood of my waterproof, a trickle finds its way inside my collar, penetrating to the rather controversial design tattooed underneath the left collarbone. Eventually a damp sensation arrives at the much-discussed embossed circle around the navel. I huddle inside my clothes and walk slowly toward the palace. If I could feel certain, after all, that my sacrifices had not been thrown away!

Now, if the people were only willing to stop at a bicep or two, I sometimes think I would go this far with no impression of duress. What can you do? I try to see it from their side of the throne, too. A certain amount has to flow from my position to their position. But there are problems of health to consider. It rains a lot in our country, and the winters are at least eight months long. Invariably, at the very lowest point of the winter, on Lower Basin Day, a delegation arrives to pay its respects from the outer reaches of the kingdom, those far-off territories where the snow never disappears from the ground, but only changes color. During their brief, hectic summer, I have been told, some angle of the sun's rays, passing through mist and ice, stains these eternal snowbanks a powerful, unnatural green. I myself have never made the trip, but I have it on authority that no one in his right mind would be taken in by the display, but no matter: the people of these remote regions are grateful even for the joke that has been played on them, they make up a few festival dances and call it summer. But you can imagine how hungry they all are for a little change in outlook and how once they arrive at the capital they are insatiable.

They have to take in all the sights: the Great Cairn, the Little Cairn, the petrified toenails of the prophet. They taste the hot sulphur springs and pocket a souvenir or two from the pile of radioactive pebbles where the Great Goose lays its eggs. Eventually a delegation arrives at the palace, requesting an audience.

You have to see them, to get the impact of my problem. The women very neatly dressed, country style, with white scarves knotted under their chins; the men in boots and leggings, with the look of shepherds or mountaineers, red-faced, gaping, presumptuous. It's taken a lot of forced courage and a bit of heavy drinking to lead up to this moment, and by now they owe it to themselves not to be turned aside. They're going to have to return to those awful snows, after all, and who knows when they'll bundle down to the capital again?

It begins respectfully enough: the women bending a knee through layers of skirts, the men reciting the salutations they've taken pains to memorize, at appropriate moments polishing the floor with their shaggy caps. But after these preliminaries come the requests. Standing in a pack to give each other courage, the women holding cupped hands over their mouths, they start with coughs, giggles, a few hints.

Then, growing bolder, they go on to some outrageous demands, a series of assaults on our royal person.

What can I do? If I give them a little finger, they're going to want a fist, if I call the palace guards and have them thrown out they'll only be ready for the next busybody who comes around with a petition for a general referendum. Politics is politics. I explain that there are effects involved that they might not care to have their wives and young daughters see. A blank stare. Those with imagination begin to suspect that there might be better reasons than they'd realized for keeping up the pressure. The others can't take in a situation more squalid or more openly inventive than the interminable winter darknesses they pass all lumped together in those tiny huts. Their daughters? Wives? They smile dimly, like children hoping not to be deprived of a promised treat.

Pleading my health, I observe that in spite of the hot geysers channeled into the pipes, for a man of my age the royal palace is not adequately heated. To make the point, I button up my bearskin jacket and plunge my hands into the pockets. The smiles broaden. His Highness must be having a good joke. They've been standing there all this time mopping their brows and furtively blotting beads of sweat from around their mouths, stifling respectfully in the unaccustomed heat. Back home, do *they* have hot-water pipes running underneath the ice? They'd like nothing better than to tear off their multilayered costumes and jump around in their plain hides.

Meanwhile, they take a step forward, their smiles widening into oafish and unpleasant grins. King or no king, they want what they've come for, and they're not going to stand around all day until it arrives. The guards are two rooms away, sleeping or gone for the afternoon. By now it seems probable that if my visitors don't succeed in stripping off my clothes, they are going to remove their own, which would be almost as disrespectful and a misdemeanor inconveniently not mentioned in any of the statutes. A compromise will have to be reached, since this is a political age.

Svendlof takes off his fur jacket, shivering a little, perfunc-
torily rolls up his shirt sleeves, and goes into the Kettle Day
act. In passing, he reminds the delegation that considerably
more of the royal carcass will be on public view on June
twelfth next year, on the occasion of the cinquennial summer sacrifice. Better reserve a seat early, as this always draws
a big crowd. If they are unable to return to the capital to
catch the spectacle, I add — finishing the act hastily, in such
poor form I am almost ashamed — they can always watch it
surrounded by their families, on their home screens. My
visitors are so delighted by the attention that they forget that
where they live the adverse magnetic conditions make reception of this or any event impossible. Let them go home and
think it over there.

Snuggled into my fur pelt, I lean back in the high tasseled
chair and watch the hushed audience file out. A bitter taste
seeps into my mouth. It was a poor show, whether they could
tell the difference or not. For the sake of the act itself, I should
have done better. I resolve never to do such a slipshod job
again, to resist all temptations to fake effects or slide by on
the strength of past performances. Remember, royalty is self-
defining. We set our own conditions.

2 Scarification

IT BEGINS WITH a childish enthusiasm, suspiciously trivial.
A small boy, already looking to the world beyond the
isthmus, spends hours down at the docks, watching the men
going about their ritualistic tasks aboard the berthed ships
of the royal navy, and finally works up the courage to ask
for a nautical sign, like theirs, on the forearm. A little anchor,
a ship's wheel, two crossed oars — nothing extreme or out-

landish, no indelible vulgarity that might be a future embarassment. Just one very small mariner's insignia.

After anxious weeks while the court consults, a favorable answer is passed down. In recognition of the seafaring traditions of the kingdom, on reaching his twelfth birthday, the boy will be permitted to acquire a plain sailor's tattoo on the left forearm. Already the word has gone out to find the best craftsmen in the line, no matter how far away. "You have three years to wait, young man. You may yet change your mind! But after you feel the pain," the boy's tutor goes on, "it's going to be too late to complain. You'll have to bear it in public without a whimper — so think it over. I wager you won't like it." The tutor yawns and scratches his ribs. "You're going to be sorry you ever started the whole silly business. You wouldn't want to go through with it a second time."

The pain, once mentioned, is forgotten, and three years pass like a dream.

Meanwhile, through all the school lessons and the lessons in ceremony, the games and the sports, runs a single thread, tightening in urgency and compulsion. At night, before sleep, possibilities are entertained: they said the twelfth birthday, but since I'm growing so fast they might push it forward to the eleventh, the tenth. Yes, they promised one very small sailor's mark, but that's only because I asked for so little. What if I put in a request for something magnificent, amazing, in several colors?

A blue-green serpent, coiled all around the arm from the wrist up to the elbow? A miniature sea battle, the smallest in the world but faithful to the last detail, pirates boarding a galleon with a broken mast and trailing sails, the desperate survivors (visible under my schoolroom magnifying glass) jumping into the shark-infested sea . . .

The golden down on the schoolboy's arm waves over the unmarked graves of the unlucky mariners; the arm flung above his head in sleep is on some nights a radiant branch of intertwining fish, flowers, butterflies, magic wheels. On others, a Wild West panorama complete with Indians, cowboys, whizzing arrows.

The twelfth birthday arrives and with it the specialist, an American recommended for his deft and hygienic performance. He brings no sinking galleons, no Wild West, no Chinese dragons, not an oar or an anchor even. Only a neat oblong, over and done with in a moment, entered into the soft flesh just under the left elbow: a little flag, our naval ensign, that familiar object I had seen flying from our mastheads since I was old enough to stand up and return a salute. "It may not be flashy, but it's good enough to last for life," the specialist grins, packing away his equipment. It is only our naval standard I am getting, after all, and *it's all in one color!*

That first time, was there pain? If so, it was less than the pain of the disappointment. The one came and went, the other lasted. Has there been pain, the many times since? That depends to some extent on the skill of the operator, the sweep of the operations. The fear of pain never held me back from drawing up my more ambitious plans, not even when weeks of protracted daily sessions lay ahead. On the other hand, during periods when faith in the scheme I had set myself drained out, when that goal seemed all purposelessness and confusion, when it appeared insane to go on yet impossible to let matters drop, then pain was what I sought out and exulted in, it gave my life shape and meaning. After a while a desensitization sets in, I suppose. Anyway, pain is supposed to be relative. Most important, for a person of my calibre I had a tough hide. So I managed on my own to give events a forceful push in the direction I knew they had to go, even if I had to wait another three years for this to happen.

At fifteen the eldest son of the royal family receives a year's training as an apprentice seaman, to prepare him for his future rank as commander of the royal navy. As an adjunct to his education, he is sent on a year's round-the-world voyage, with stopovers at major ports. Fortunately, our kingdom, because of the disparity of climate and produce, keeps up trading ties with several Oriental countries.

I came home from that first trip with a number of personal accretions that could not be rubbed off or washed away; hasty one-session jobs picked up in the back room of obscure parlors while my shipmates acted as lookouts and our whistle let off steam in the harbor, urging speed. Some of these jobs have a spontaneity and charm that I treasure to this day. Others I have had worked over or incorporated into larger designs. But a beginning had been made. The crown prince Svendlof came home with five new tattoos, one moderately obscene.

This calamity – or commitment, depending on how you look at it – had the court in upheaval for weeks. Officers were called to account, and the captain of our ship was relieved of his command. But what can you do? How do you keep an active young chap, even a king's son, under day-and-night surveillance? Bad companions led him into bad ways. Luckily, the most questionable memento was on a part of the future king's anatomy that would be uncovered only to intimates.

At this time, it was decided that more attention ought to be given to my religious training, and to this incentive I owe some of my most inspired and moving effects. Religious symbolism, I found later, had a way of drawing the best work from the operators, and at that susceptible stage of my own development, I came on religion hard.

The broad-minded young monk who was my counselor was pleased when he came into the suite we shared and found me sketching borders of crosses, crescents, Stars of David, Arabic dots for warding off the evil eye, Aztec suns, the moons of Diana. . . . At that time I took an interest in heraldry. Then I began going to museums, searched down old prints and reproductions of the world's great paintings. The monk disappeared from my life, and I was allowed to enroll in the royal art academy, where I developed my lifelong admiration for painted Greek pottery, marveling at how adroitly the great, often unknown artist related his designs to the contours and modeling of the vessel.

And finally, I went in for a strenuous program of Indian exercises and muscle building. After years of practice I could flex and undulate large groups of muscles at will (already visualizing the tasks they would be called on to perform). All this moving toward when the time was ripe, and I could call my life my own.

Now that my work is nearly complete, now that I am a much-photographed celebrity, now that popular songs about me have been sung and writhed to by millions from London to Murmansk, now that our kingdom has become a household word from the Khasi Hills to the Azores, now that I have done what I could for my people, breaking through centuries of narrowness and suspicion, opening their lives to a touch of the European humanistic tradition – if I had to do it again, how would I go about it differently? Not the details, the small half-aware choices and random mistakes we slide into: but the basic, unalterable decisions?

I must admit that many times I have wished to be able to start out fresh and choose all over again, but what is done is done. With the exception of about four square inches at the back of the right thigh I am covered from earlobe to toenail, my skin has been worked over and embellished down to the spaces between my fingers and my toes. . . . With only enough area untouched on my face, so I should not appear an absolute monster. . . . My ministers and advisers, who were horrified when they realized how far I intended to go talked of having me declared incompetent and reconsidered only when the people showed enthusiasm for this project of their young king and agitation for an end to the royal house died down. Indeed, the people were behind me from the start, not only the steps I introduced for more rational and enlightened governmental policies, but – in the other direction – they enthusiastically took up my efforts to revive the old noble customs and practices, fallen into disuse.

I personally reintroduced the Great Kettle Day ceremony, injecting the royal presence as a tangy component. I set into motion the delicate machinery that brought back the Summer Sacrifice on June twelfth, the longest day of the year according to Old Calendar. This ancient ceremony, traditionally held every fifth year, had been nearly forgotten owing to the degenerate custom on which it was founded, about which the least said the better. Nowadays, refurbished and cleaned up, our midsummer spectacular is a noisy success with the thousands that it attracts, swamping our limited touristic facilities, and with the millions in every part of the globe who participate owing to the wonders of an advanced technology.

Apart from these official appearances, my vocation has isolated me and turned me in on myself. Before matters went as far as they did, at least I mingled with the public on occasion, but now that everyone, to the smallest child, can recognize me on sight, I prefer to avoid the boring formalities raised by these encounters and keep pretty much to the palace grounds. Marriage, in spite of the urgings of my advisers, I never seriously considered. Women are such notorious rearrangers of décor, a wife would never have been willing to let well enough alone but would have been after me to change this, change that; revise the color scheme, ruin the outline by finicky overelaboration, censor the more piquant details – so I never could take the risk.

Though, who knows? The advice of another person of taste and judgment might have been valuable. In carrying out my scheme, it's possible that I went too far or not far enough. Although I searched out the best Japanese and Burmese craftsmen, submitting for weeks or months at a stretch to the prodding of their little ivory needles, dipped in indigo, saffron, rose madder, even these masters could not give more than I originally asked. Too hesitant or too fluctuating, at the beginning, to think in terms of a single, overriding assault, I tried a bit of everything, attempted to do justice to every subject and possibility . . . leaving me this scrawl of fragments and details, some beautiful, some merely curious, some reflecting my travels, some my reading, scenes from the history of my people and reminders of what they would rather forget.

Oh, I see, now, that as time goes on I will have less and less to offer. The colors grow muddy and sink in, the realignment of tissue and muscle alters my most carefully thoughtout projects. The deterioration of the early work is plain to those who care to look. A new generation will shrug, and take for granted what their parents approached with veneration and delight. Which is why I am especially sorry that tomorrow, at what should be the pinnacle of his career, Svendlof will not dazzle the people with a new and brilliant invention on the small area he has been holding in reserve.

Some ravishing consummation, some prodigy never before approached in our isolated kingdom or the great world beyond. . . . It's become harder and harder to let go of that last statement. Those few blank inches on the right leg are the last free space left to me, and I can't make up my mind to close up shop, and be done for good. What to choose, anyway, when you've covered almost every subject known to civilized man? And after choosing, what then?

The people will be mildly disappointed when we climb up on the wooden platform tomorrow, and they see we have nothing new to offer. They will have to be patient and indulge their old king for another five years. Some effects just cannot be forced. Time shortens, all kinds of doubts are creeping in. Possibly that one unworked area is all that I have left to hold on to. After the pain and the dislocation, what was it supposed to mean? Who is this Svendlof, or who was he? Perhaps a different, a less demanding sort of life. . . . Too often, lately, I stop and ask, where does the needle end, where does Svendlof begin? Fortunately, there is still this little clear space left.

3   Sacrifice

GOOD AFTERNOON, LADIES and gentlemen. Here we are, at the opening of the very special ceremony held once every five years in this little kingdom. Crowds are gathered from all over the world. I see a number of young people carrying knapsacks who look like they've been hitchhiking or sleeping in the fields. And yes, there are the more conventional tourists, who are making the pilgrimage up to this remote spot, some for the first time but others coming back like clockwork every five years. It's a very popular and colorful pageant they hold up here, and I don't think it's in poor taste to mention that their greatly admired king, Svendlof – that's s-v-e-n-d-l-o-f, only one f – is getting on in years, and we don't know how many more opportunities there will be for viewing this spectacle, as he organized it.

They are setting up the preparations in the square down below – that's the capital's main square we are looking down on, it may not seem very imposing, but that is the main cattle market, with the wooden cows' heads sticking out, to the right, and beyond that, the low timbered building with the banners flying – that's the town hall. Then, you can just see the towers over the tops of the trees to the far left, that is the royal residence, from which the king, Svendlof, should be making his way in about ten minutes.

While we're here waiting, we'd like to fill you in a little
on the general atmosphere, what it feels like to be a visitor
from overseas, descending into what you might think of as
another world. First, not only is this national capital about
the size of a small town back home, but this is actually a
very small country, smaller than you might expect. Our pilot
informed us that at normal cruising speed he can cover it
end to end in about twenty minutes, and when we landed,
to give you an idea, there were herds of reindeer grazing over
the turf, a kind of tundra, in the middle of which the very
new and experimentally designed airport terminal suddenly
rises up. When you see those permanent ice caps at the north-
ern border and down here, in the southern part, these brows-
ing caribou and reindeer, with a small boy in charge to shoo
them off the landing strip — well, you begin to think you're
stepping right into Santa's workshop.

Down below now, the carpenters are banging away putting the final touches on a sort of wooden scaffolding or platform. It somewhat resembles a prizefighter's ring, except it's
pretty high off the ground, no doubt to give the crowds a
full view of the activities, and there are the same protective
ropes as around a boxer's ring. Now the carpenters have left,
and a beautiful red cloth is being draped inside the platform
and down the tall stairs leading to it. This cloth or carpeting
will run the full length, about three city blocks, to the palace,
along the route which the king is expected to travel.

This is a very important day for this tiny kingdom, and
fortunately it's a good day. The sun is shining. It is June
twelfth, which according to the Old Calendar marked the
longest day in the year. We are close enough to the summer
solstice for there to be hardly any night, just an hour or two
of twilight from about midnight to two A.M. But consider-
ing all those hours of sunshine piling up, it's still a nippy
day for June. As you see, I'm wearing my topcoat, and I have
to mention Bill Evans, over the way, has refused to take off

his muffler and gloves. Yes, we all have to agree, it's going to take old-fashioned grit and endurance today to go through with what their king, Svendlof, is going to do.

Now the square is beginning to crowd up, and the scene is getting that much livelier. In addition to the townsfolk, people seem to have converged on the capital from all over the country, in many cases bringing their herds with them, driving them into the pens of the cattle market, here on the main square. Apparently there's going to be some kind of livestock auction after the official ceremony. You can hear the lowing or the bleating of the animals coming through pretty strong, over the sounds of people excitedly milling about. By now the inhabitants of the country appear to outnumber the overseas visitors by, say, a ratio of eight or nine to one, and more are arriving. They're generally in a pretty happy mood. Some may be slightly too happy – here's a man throwing his picturesque shaggy skin cap in the air, and a number of men are fighting and pushing their way toward it. The owner of the hat has disappeared under those diving bodies, there may be a certain danger, but no, the owner has his hat back on, and he's being lifted by the crowd, being given a very bumpy ride, but he's grinning and seems to enjoy it, tossed from one man's shoulders to the next.

You may notice that during this little melee a number of the foreign visitors, carrying their cameras and tripods, have retreated, made their way back from the center of the crowd to a spot underneath the porticoes of the town hall. For an official ceremony, with crowds like these, it might appear unusual that there are no guards or policemen anywhere to be seen. It's one of their traditions that these independent people, in spite of their king who is a sort of national symbol or figurehead, have been a completely self-governing unit for the past thousand years or more. And they do manage to work out their own problems, as in the case of the man, before, who seemed in danger of being trampled.

This actually is a pretty strange, fairly quaint sort of place. You might call it a study in contrasts. While we are waiting for more activity to develop out there – the crowd is getting slightly restless, people are looking around toward the palace, some are stamping their feet and whistling – while we are still waiting, we might try to fill you in on some of those contrasts or extremes, as they appeared to us while we were being driven from the airport to the central square of the capital, where we are now set up on a second-floor balcony of the first-class hotel.

To begin, it hits you how little there is to work with, in the way of natural resources. The main product of the country seems to be stones, pebbles, and volcanic rock. Nevertheless, the occupants seem comfortable and cheerful in their neat houses made of rough-hewn stone, sort of a hive-shaped cairn with twigs or moss sticking out between. Like people all over the world, they make the best of what they have. In front of nearly every house, you'll see a few potted plants and pebbles raked up very neatly. In addition, all along that main highway, nearly every house we passed had one or more antennas up on top, indicating that those within were in touch with the outer world, no matter how cut off or backward they might seem.

Naturally, not knowing the language, we of the press contingent couldn't respond to the greetings shouted from doorways as we passed. However, what was surprising was how the children ran after the cars and tried to encircle our motorcade as it made its way up that very rough main artery. At some spots where the road turned or narrowed, they got in front of the lead car, where they joined hands and stopped us from moving forward.

To be frank, we had to put up quite a struggle to keep these very peppy, mischievous country kids from climbing up and breaking off whatever could be removed – windshield wipers, side mirrors, radio antennas – cutting strips off the tops of the convertibles, even pulling at our clothing. . . . Your reporter, as a result of an encounter, lost his glasses – fortunately I always carry a spare. Though I wonder how that little rascal feels, running around with a stranger's glasses on his face!

Well, well, some action seems to be shaping up down below. Here comes the town crier, that fellow in the romantic outfit, a skin cape with maybe a thousand animal tails attached to it. He really is quite a sight. That's an animal horn he is blowing, it's a loud raucous sound, and it seems to jolt the people awake. They're beginning to shout and make a lot of noise. And here is their king now. Here he comes, making his way down the long, very red runner.

Yes, King Svendlof is striding down that scarlet carpet! And his highness really has a remarkable appearance. It's most remarkable. You'll notice he has on a magnificent fur robe, it's fastened high under the ears and trails the ground as he walks. It's a dark brown fur, very lustrous. And then you have those straight white locks descending almost to his shoulders but cut high across the forehead. Except for the white hair, you'd hardly think of his highness as an older person. He has great command and power in the way he places one foot after the other, moving up the red strip.

You'll observe that the face of his majesty has numerous marks, in several colors and designs, outlining the short bangs on his forehead, appearing above the jawline, and bordering the cheeks. Although you realize the king was – and still is – a handsome man, you get the impression that a second face has been superimposed over his real one. It's an odd sensation, a bit of a double take.

The crowds are responding very strongly to the presence of their king. He is obviously a very popular figure in this little kingdom. You can see the affection in which young and old hold him. There's a lot of jumping up and down and shouting his name. Through it all, Svendlof keeps coming down that carpet. He has reached the scaffolding in the center of the square, and before ascending he turns and holds up a hand in a royal salute. You see how the hand is absolutely covered with these patterns and figures, giving you an idea of the situation underneath the fur robe.

More and more people are shouting his name, you can hear it coming through in their peculiar accent – "Svendlof! Svendlof!" – and the king is just starting to climb that little carpeted staircase.

He is moving more slowly. The crowd might be described as getting a little out of hand. Some of the men have taken off their characteristic tufted fur hats, and have sent them flying toward the stage, and other men are diving after them, repeating in this very dense crowd the scene we witnessed earlier. There is a certain agitation and rolling movement out there, as people raise their hands high, to throw hats or other objects, and their neighbors stoop, diving after what has been thrown. You can hear an occasional shriek, probably from a woman or child. But over it, that penetrating invocation: Svendlof, Svendlof.

And now his highness has reached the platform. He climbs over the ropes, stands still for a moment, and then he flings his arms wide and tosses the fur robe into a corner.

I tell you, this is strong stuff! The king has taken off his royal robes and is standing there with no protection in this cool, rather breezy weather for June. You have this statuesque, strong-looking human body, and yet it is not a human body. . . . That is, I don't know if this is a human body I see before me or a wallpaper sample. It's covered with design. It's not easy to make out the components, except that lower down, where you normally expect some clothing, the patterns are so worked-over and run together, you get a shadowlike effect. It's as if his highness had put on a pair of bathing trunks – there's no feeling of exposure or impropriety.

And now his highness is turning around, and we detect high on his back this rather blurry picture: a young girl being molested by a swan, or maybe it's a young boy being attacked by an eagle. I think you can make out that as his highness moves, undulating his shoulder, he is causing this eagle's – or swan's – wings to flutter, to rise and fall. It is truly a fascinating performance he's putting on. This Svendlof is quite a showman, and he's right in there with his audience.

And now we can see that going all the way down to his heels, the entire back of his majesty is covered with pictures, and he's animating them, shifting from one set of muscles to another. You have to marvel at his development and control. There he is, animating these little images he carries on his body – see that old-fashioned sailing ship rocking in a gale! – until he gets down to a white spot, it seems a patch of natural skin on the upper right thigh, which shines out against the darkened and colored areas around it.

This particular spot looks as if someone had forgotten to finish the job or had given up before it was completed. It makes for a rather patchy effect. Whatever the reason, I'd say this was the one flaw in a very impressive and otherwise almost perfect achievement.

And now the people are beginning to show their thanks for this performance of their good king. The clapping, foot stomping, and whistles are getting heavier and shriller. Is my voice still coming through? Our wooden balcony is beginning to sway from the vibrations. *Lend me a hand, and hold down these cables, will you?* Well, as we said, the crowd is giving Svendlof a tremendous ovation. In fact, at this minute a few enthusiasts, young men in those shaggy fur headpieces, are stepping out of the mob and running up the red-carpeted staircase.

They're ducking under the ropes, and onto the platform. It seems they want to congratulate their king face to face.

They want to touch him, slap him on the back, run their hands over his body. Svendlof is taking it well. He's stepping back a little, but he's smiling, he's good-humoredly accepting these rather vigorous tributes.

And now more men – and women too – are stepping out of the crowd and swarming up the carpeted staircase. You get this sizable crowd, full of personal adulation, maybe a little uncontrolled, and nobody around to regulate or hold down their movements. Let me tell you, I wouldn't want to be in this Svendlof's shoes right now, though he's accepted the buffeting in good grace. Nothing seems to disturb him. . . . He keeps smiling but backing up, as more and more of his subjects arrive.

And now a new development – something new seems to be taking place on that platform. Ladies and gentlemen, yes, it seems that King Svendlof has taken a fall in stepping back from his admirers. He has fallen or tripped but apparently has not been injured. He has recovered his footing and is leaning back against a rope at this moment. He is still smiling, but he seems tired, out of breath. By now he must be wishing his adulators would tone down their enthusiasm and leave, and it's certainly time they did. But they are still demonstrating their rather frantic devotion, leaning over their king, who is pressed back flat against the ropes.

And now something new and tremendous does seem to be happening out there! We can't be sure – but yes, a knife. We see a knife or possibly a number of knives. Can Svendlof be in danger from an overexcited subject? Why doesn't anybody come to his assistance? Where are his helpers and loyal followers?

The king appears to be making no effort to defend himself from what looks like an onslaught of knives. It's a little difficult seeing what is being attempted, but no – oh, no – these men must be mad. They are, they are digging in with these knives, and they are taking pieces of skin off a living man. Can't anybody stop them? My God, these people must be insane, they are cutting away his skin. . . . Ladies and gentlemen, these savages are digging in and seemingly flaying their old king, Svendlof. WON'T ANYBODY STOP THEM?

I am being stripped, I am being slowly peeled free of myself. I see myself slide free, like a snake that's burst useless skin. What need for it any more?

Pieces of my hide, still dripping, are being carried away like trophies. They pass from hand to hand, they are held up like banners.

Everyone wants a share — too many out there are straining forward. There is danger of trampling, of suffocation.

Let no one go away unsatisfied. Let each take what is his. Tell the people not to push or crowd, there will be enough to go around and to spare.